CONFUSI
LOVE
WITH OBSESSION

D0283777

CONFUSING LOVE WITH OBSESSION

When Being in Love
Means Being in Control

Third Edition

JOHN D. MOORE

HAZELDEN

Hazelden
Center City, Minnesota 55012-0176

1-800-328-0094
1-651-213-4590 (Fax)
www.hazelden.org

©2002, 2004, 2006 by John D. Moore
Originally published by iUniverse, Inc., as *Confusing Love with Obsession: When You Can't Stop Controlling Your Partner and the Relationship*
Third edition published by Hazelden in 2006
Printed in the United States of America

Library of Congress Cataloging-in-Publication Data
Moore, John D., 1970–
    Confusing love with obsession : when being in love means being in
control / John D. Moore. —3rd ed.
        p. cm.
    Includes bibliographical references and index.
    ISBN-13: 978-1-59285-356-4
    ISBN-10: 1-59285-356-0
    1. Relationship addiction. 2. Obsessive-compulsive disorder.
3. Control (Psychology) 4. Addicts—Rehabilitation. I. Title.

RC552.R44M66 2006
616.85'84—dc22

                                                2006043571

Author's note

All of the discussions, case histories, and stories contained in this book are based on actual experiences. To protect the privacy and identity of the people involved, names and details have been changed. In some cases, composites have been created.

This book is intended to help people who may be suffering from an addiction to relationships and are seeking information as it relates to recovery. The information contained herein should be used for informational purposes only. Readers are encouraged to research the issue of relationship addictions and discuss any possible concerns with their health care providers.

10 09   6 5 4 3 2

Cover design by David Spohn
Interior design by Ann Sudmeier
Typesetting by Prism Publishing Center

For my mother:
You passed away a few short months before
the publication of *Confusing Love with Obsession*.
I will always love you.

To my brother Frank:
I am a part of you, and you are a part of me.

To the overworked and underpaid human service worker:
The work you do is important.

To those who suffer silently:
You are not alone.

CONTENTS

ACKNOWLEDGMENTS

WORDS CANNOT EXPRESS my sincere, heartfelt gratitude for the people who helped me make this book a reality. I first wish to thank Quinn Tyler Jackson who patiently read through everything I *ever* sent him and offered his feedback in a caring and supportive manner. On the days I thought I would never get through this project, he was a source of comfort and compassion.

I would also like to thank Robert Donato for being a loving friend. Whenever I wanted to bounce a particular point of concept off Bob, he was there to listen—even as late as three o'clock in the morning. He truly helped me shape the direction of this book and is a walking saint.

Another helping friend was Joe Phillips, who read each chapter of my manuscript and made the necessary corrections to my grammar. Eager to help and always supportive, Joe helped me to see things I could not. He is a truly wonderful person and gifted human being.

Finally, I wish to thank all of the people who shared their personal trials and tribulations. You have helped to shed light on a problem that does not get better over time.

SHELTER FROM THE STORM
An Introduction

> Any building that has stood firm, surviving the great
> disaster undamaged still has its roof drowned by the
> highest waves, and its towers buried below the flood.
> And now the land and sea are not distinct,
> all is the sea—a sea without a shore.
>
> —Ovid, *The Metamorphoses*

WE HAVE FEARED STORMS since the beginning. During early years, our species huddled in caves, pieced together flimsy shelters made of sticks and animal skins, and hid under cliffs for protection from the sky. When ominous storm clouds collided on the horizon, we prayed to ancient gods to shield us from nature's fury.

As decades turned into centuries, we advanced technologically and learned to craft stronger, mightier shelters made of concrete and glass, daring the storms to take their best shot.

Today, our homes are weatherproof and, for the most part, save us from the sky's wrath. At this very moment, satellites are in continuous orbit above our world, scanning the planet for signs of trouble and warning us of pending atmospheric doom. We rejoice each time we escape a storm's rage and feel relieved when the threat of destruction has passed.

Indeed, on those occasions when we have triumphed over the storm, *we were in control.*

But sometimes, despite the warnings signs, storm clouds collide and destroy our "weatherproof" homes, crushing them with fantastic, intense power. When this happens, we arrive at the stark realization that *control was just an illusion.* In our grief, we examine the damage to others and ourselves and ask the question, "Why?" Left helpless and alone in a sea of destruction and sorrow, we choke back painful tears and cry out to God, "How could this happen?" and "What do I do now?"

You see, it is not the storm itself we fear but the aftermath of what it leaves behind.

For some of us, being in a personal relationship is like trying to control a powerful, destructive storm. It is a cruel, never-ending battle that requires every ounce of energy to wage. Tragically, however, no matter how much we try to exert control over the storm, it *always* wins.

When being in a relationship means needing to be in control, we are *confusing love with obsession.* When we pathologically obsess over our partner's whereabouts, we are confusing love with obsession. When we refuse to let her have any friends and are constantly monitoring her, we are confusing love with obsession. When we make her quit her job or do not let her work at all, fearing possible infidelity, we are confusing love with obsession. When we believe we can stop his abusive ways by changing our behavior, we are confusing love with obsession. When we can't sleep at night because our minds are on *him,* we are confusing love with obsession. When we keep him overweight or refuse to let him exercise, we are confusing love with obsession. When we use money as a tool to chain her to the relationship, we are confusing love with obsession. When we use drugs, alcohol, and sex as a way of coping with the pain in our relationships, we are confusing love with obsession. And when we feel that we cannot live without our partner, we are absolutely confusing love with obsession.

You may be reading this book because you are confusing love with obsession. Quite possibly, you are reading this book because you have learned that your significant other has been cheating, and you want to manipulate the situation to your advantage. Or maybe you are tired of obsessively worrying over your partner's whereabouts and are emotionally and physically drained. Perhaps you are living with a partner who has become unbearable, controlling every part of your life. For all of these reasons, *you are hurting.* In a place where darkness rules, it is hard to focus on today.

This book is not about *getting over it.* Only a fool thinks deep pain is something that can be waved away with a magic wand. The suffering each of us has endured is personal and unique, with its own individuality. It has taken years to learn the art of controlling people, and the energy we have expended has probably caused immeasurable sorrow. The same can be said of the persons being controlled—as their lives often define the word *suffering.* Pain is a part of who we are, serving as a reminder that we are indeed vulnerable. If pain is left alone to fester inside, however, it gains energy like a powerful storm and eventually overpowers us.

People who do not understand the struggles of those who confuse love with obsession try to help by offering words of support. More often, however, these words are like swords through the heart, reminding us that our secret pain cannot be easily cured. How many times have we heard a friend or loved one say, "You'll get over it" or "Everything will be okay"? My own personal favorite is, "You really need to bring closure to this." What they do not realize is that closure implies an ending, but for many of us, ending is not part of our vocabulary.

This book is about those of us who are addicted to our relationships and will do anything to stop our partner from leaving us—in other words, those of us who confuse love with obsession. We will examine the typical traits, characteristics, and behaviors of people who confuse love with obsession and uncover the causal factors behind this insidious form of relational addiction.

Essentially what we will be exploring in this publication is a combination of what the American Psychiatric Association refers to in the *Diagnostic and Statistical Manual of Mental Disorders (DSM-IV-TR, or DSM)* as dependent personality disorder and borderline personality disorder. While all of the behaviors of people who confuse love with obsession may not fit neatly into these *DSM* diagnoses, they closely reflect what we will be exploring. That stated, *please avoid the temptation of self-diagnosing,* as people who confuse love with obsession often exhibit diagnostic criteria from various *DSM*-related conditions.

Don't be frightened by the words *dependent, disorder, addiction,* and particularly *addict.* The typical, media-influenced stereotypes of people who suffer from such concerns are, at best, exaggerated and, at worse, false. The truth is, "addicts" are not fully understood, primarily because they are commonly defined by their addiction rather than by whom they are as people. We need to ask ourselves, Is a woman who happens to be addicted to alcohol *just* an alcoholic or is she more—such as a mother, wife, sister, or friend? As you read this book, try to focus on the concepts and experiences presented herein and try to erase any preconceptions about what it means to be addicted. You will find it easier to grasp the general concepts and to recognize your own behaviors. Furthermore, the words *addiction, dependent,* and *obsessive* are used interchangeably throughout this book as a means of describing certain behaviors.

I became aware of people who confuse love with obsession several years ago when I joined a support group for the relationally addicted. In time, I became a sponsor to others in the group, helping them through various crises, while offering help and support whenever and wherever I could. It was then that I began to realize that several group members were employing certain tactics in their relationships because of an overwhelming need to control their partner. Motivated by curiosity, I began to research and investigate the causal reasons behind this problem through personal interviews and then started sharing my findings with others.

As a former case manager in the social services field and now a psychotherapist, I have seen the devastating effects of relational dependency in the lives of many clients. I have also seen these same effects in people attending various addiction support groups and trying to embark down a path to healing. But more important, I have experienced the horrific damage of this addiction in my own life—you see, *I* am a person who confuses love with obsession. I have learned that recovery from such an addiction is an ongoing process, and part of recovery means sharing knowledge and experiences with others, like you. In other words, I have lived it.

This book is filled with insight from people who suffer from this addiction, with stories from the human perspective. Their stories, coupled with clinical interpretations, help us understand why we behave in certain ways in our relationships—ways that seem normal to us.

This book is for woman *and* men, because both sexes deal with this problem. While we may fool ourselves into thinking that only women deal with an addiction to their relationships or with an obsession for another person—quite the opposite is true. People who confuse love with obsession can be of *any* gender, age, or sexual orientation and come from all walks of life. And to be sure, the problem of confusing love with obsession has become exacerbated due to unhealthy societal messages. In our culture, we are taught early on that being involved in a personal relationship is an absolute *must* and that the woman or man attached to our arm represents a sign of success and somehow validates us.

The ideas and information contained in the following chapters should be thought of as guidelines and spiritual lessons. Some of the stories may be painful or even embarrassing to read because they speak to your current situation. When this happens, put the book aside for a little while and pick it up again later. Although every chapter in this book may not relate specifically to your experience, it's helpful to read each of them to understand various addictive patterns. The people, experiences, and case studies presented in this book come from a series of personal discussions with people from support groups, clients, friends, and others who have contacted me through various means. As with all addictions, there are faces behind the clinical name. Some of the stories may seem wild, even unreal, but they are all true. You will get the most out of this book if you read it carefully and revisit chapters often. The names of people and some details have been changed to protect identities. Because of the nature of relational dependency and all of the various ways we can exert control over another, it was simply not possible to list and explore every possible method in this publication. What follows are some of the more common, yet insidious, methods that we can use to manipulate a partner and an examination of how, in the final analysis, their employment wreaks great heartache and pain on all parties involved. By identifying these methods and recognizing how we might be destructively using them in our personal situations, we can take the first steps on the path of healing. It is not a book for the faint of heart, and I know it may be difficult to read.

I hope this book sheds light on the daily struggles you may live with. *You are not alone.* If just one person is helped with this publication, then the goal has been accomplished.

1

WHEN BEING IN LOVE
MEANS BEING IN CONTROL

*In dreams last night, the heavens and the earth poured out
great groans while I alone stood facing devastation.*

—*The Epic of Gilgamesh*

HEART POUNDING, stomach churning, Nancy walked into
my home that warm summer evening with a stunned look on
her face. She appeared disoriented and unfocused, her entire
body shaking. As I motioned her toward my living room, she
said, "I'm sorry to be bothering you, but the unthinkable has
happened. What am I going to do?"

Because I was her designated sponsor in a support group
for the relationally addicted, it was my responsibility to offer
help during times of crisis. I had only known her for a few
weeks and was still trying to understand her needs. When
she had called earlier that day requesting to meet, I knew that
something serious had happened, given the desperate tone of
her voice.

From my chair, I observed her sitting quietly on a nearby
couch. Everything about Nancy appeared fragile; she was pe-
tite and underweight, with pale, white skin and straight black
hair that was fading into something between brown and gray.
For a thirty-seven-year-old housewife, she looked much older
than her years. She focused her dark brown eyes on the
Chicago skyline, visible through the window of my high-rise

apartment. Without making eye contact, she asked if she could smoke.

The room became silent for a few moments while she lit her cigarette and inhaled deeply.

"I cannot believe the bastard would do this to me," she said in a raspy voice, trying to choke back tears. "How could this happen? We have been married for twelve years, and I *never* thought Ron would sleep around on me, let alone pay for another woman's rent." She turned her head in my direction. "I thought things had been going so well. We just celebrated our anniversary two weeks ago. He was going to take me to Mexico later this month as a gift."

Her next words were measured and deliberate. "What the hell is wrong with me? Am I ugly or something?" She extinguished her cigarette in an ashtray and immediately lit a new one.

"I am going to beat the shit out of her when I get my hands on that bitch. I found out where she lives, you know. I plan on going over there to get her." She shook her head and ground her teeth. "Oh, she will pay for this! What kind of a woman would involve herself with a married man? I had a feeling something was going on, and I got the proof last night," she yelled, her eyes welling with tears. "My worst fears have come true."

Nancy went on to explain the particulars of how she had learned of her husband's betrayal, detailing the events from the night before. She had been keeping a constant eye on the clock, becoming more anxious with each passing hour. When he was not home from work by ten at night, she decided to find out why.

"I called him at his office fourteen times between five-thirty and nine and got no answer," she explained. "I found out the truth about his whereabouts from his cell phone."

Based on her story, I could almost envision her hellish discovery. Earlier that morning while her husband was taking a shower, she had secretly looked through his wallet and obtained the password to his cell phone. When he wasn't home by ten, she decided to use her newfound information and dialed the number to disaster. What she heard was indeed shocking.

"It's Denise, babe. Thanks for dropping off the rent check. I cannot wait until you get divorced so we can share the apartment together. I love you!" said a cheery, younger voice on his cell phone's voice mail.

Nancy started to open up now, talking about the situation with increasing vigor. "I am just so angry for allowing this to happen. Ron is such a good-looking man. I should have known that some lowlife would try and take him away. I cannot get the image of him and another woman out of my mind. The thought of him laughing, kissing, and making love with her is infuriating," she said, using one of the tissues I had offered to wipe away the black mascara that was running down her face.

"Ron has been working late hours in the past few months, but I never thought anything of it." I wondered how truthful Nancy was being here. She looked away for a moment and then continued to sing her sad song.

"Actually, he has always worked late, but I could usually track him down if needed. But something weird happened last month that set off alarm bells. He was going to Miami on a business trip and did not offer to take me along." She clutched the tissues in her fist. "I usually go on trips to Florida with him, you know, as a kind of vacation." She twitched her nose. "But he didn't want to take me, using some excuse about it being a short trip and that I wouldn't have any fun. I begged him to take me, but he wasn't interested."

She went on to explain how lonely she had felt while he was gone, experiencing anxiety from the moment he left for the airport.

"So there I was, all alone while he flew to Miami. I was in total misery while he was gone. When I would call him at his hotel, he was *never* there, even at two o'clock in the morning. I must have smoked three packs of cigarettes each day that he was gone. All I could do was think about where he was, who he was talking to, and who he might be with. Trying to sleep at night was impossible; you get used to someone next to you in the bed, you know?"

In her grief, she struggled to remain focused. After a few moments of tearful reflection, she continued telling her story.

"When he returned home from the trip, he acted completely different. He avoided me as much as possible and started sleeping on the couch. If I tried to seduce him, he pushed me away. I felt so rejected. After awhile, I knew something was going on—something terribly wrong."

Indeed, Nancy had known that *something* was wrong with her marriage for quite some time. I wondered how her behavior toward Ron during their marriage might have influenced her current situation.

She continued to talk. "After I heard Denise's voice mail yesterday, I searched through Ron's private e-mail on his laptop and found her telephone number. They've been writing love notes back and forth like two teenagers." Her next words were troublesome. "I've already called the bimbo's house five times, but I haven't left a message—*yet*. I used the block-caller-ID feature, so she can't identify me." She said this with a smile on her face, apparently gaining satisfaction at having control over the caller ID box in Denise's home.

There was a short period of silence. She lit a new cigarette.

"Okay, if I am going to really be honest with you, I guess

I better tell you that this wasn't the first time I caught him cheating. A couple of years ago, I found out Ron was sleeping with another woman from work. It was some telephone sales agent in another department—the tramp."

"How did you handle the situation back then?" I asked.

Nancy produced a weak but prideful grin. "I got her fired. Ron's company values customer service, you know." She exhaled a cloud of smoke. "Amazing how a few well-placed telephone calls to someone's boss can wreak havoc upon them."

She went on to explain that she had called the woman's supervisor repeatedly, each time disguising her voice and pretending to be a different person. After hearing half a dozen complaints about the employee's telephone etiquette, the supervisor decided to terminate her employment.

"I got the bitch canned!" she concluded, her grin transforming into a full-fledged smile.

That Nancy would go to such harmful and unhealthy lengths to keep Ron from leaving her for another woman indicated a serious addiction to their marriage. For people who confuse love with obsession, however, her behavior was not that uncommon.

"What are you planning on doing about the current situation?" I asked.

"After I curse out this *Denise* on the phone, I plan on doing something very nasty to her—far worse than what I did to Ron's first mistress." She looked up toward the ceiling in a thoughtful manner. "Maybe I'll slash her tires." She paused to reconsider. "No, I'll get her personal information and then order some credit cards in her name. I deserve a few new outfits after what *they* have put me through. I can ruin that bitch's financial life and let Ron be the jerk to foot her bills. We'll see how far those rent checks go when they bounce into next week." But her next words were even more alarming.

"It won't be the first time I have done something behind Ron's back to keep him from leaving. We had the boys because I tricked him."

"What do you mean?" I asked.

"From the very first moment I met Ron, I knew I wanted to be with him forever. So when we first started dating, I told him that I was on birth control. Little did he know that the *pill* he saw me taking was nothing more than a vitamin."

I started to imagine the early days of their courtship. Nancy was younger and attractive, and Ron was woefully naive to her obsessive ways. I could see them both going out for a "night on the town," eventually capping off their evening with wild, passionate sex. With each new sexual encounter, Nancy knew that she stood a good chance of becoming pregnant.

"To this day, he doesn't know the truth about how I got pregnant. I told him that 'sometimes the Pill doesn't work.' I even showed him an informational brochure to prove it," she said.

Nancy became more reflective.

"You know, I guess I should have seen this coming all along. The more I tried to control Ron, the further he slipped away. Why does this always happen to me?" Her eyes welled again with tears. "Everyone I have ever loved has left me, even my boys." She was now looking directly at me. "I should have told you that my two sons moved in with Ron's parents last week. We never really got along because they said I was too controlling. Can you believe that? A bunch of ungrateful assholes, I tell you." I probed her for more details.

"Whenever the kids would get out of line, I would punish them—you know, take away their privileges. Other times I would just scream at them."

"And if that didn't work?" I asked.

"Then I would hit them." She lowered her head. "Looking back, I guess that I was pretty mean to them. I wish things would just return back to normal—the way things used to be. I've got to get Ron back. I know I can. He still loves me, doesn't he? What am I going to do now?"

So why was Nancy so obsessed with Ron? Why, for example, did she become instantly attached to him so early in their relationship? Why did she manipulate her pregnancy and, for that matter, him? And why did she engage in acts of revenge against the women whom he was having affairs with? Is there an explanation for the abuse that she directed toward her children? How did her past influence her present?

Nearly all of Nancy's behaviors are common for people who believe that being in love means being in control. One thing is for certain. Becoming a person who confuses love with obsession does not happen randomly. In fact, the clues to this phenomenon can be traced to the past, where childhood memories that should be filled with love and support are instead filled with loneliness, fear, and deep sorrow. The following traits, characteristics, and behaviors are common among people who confuse love with obsession.

COMMON TRAITS, CHARACTERISTICS, AND BEHAVIORS OF PEOPLE WHO CONFUSE LOVE WITH OBSESSION

1. We were emotionally abandoned and may have been verbally, psychologically, or physically abused (or all three) during childhood.
2. We trap partners into relationships by withholding emotions or finances, or through other means of manipulation.
3. We engage in acts of revenge against people we perceive as a threat to our relationships.

4. We are constantly preoccupied with our significant other's whereabouts, spending most of the day monitoring and tracking her physical and financial moves.
5. We restrict a partner's ability to communicate with and/or have friends.
6. We use food as a way of keeping a partner overweight, hoping that he will appear unattractive and thus undesirable to others.
7. We may be coaddicted to alcohol, other drugs, food, or sex.
8. Our worst fear is being abandoned, and we will do *anything* to stop a partner from leaving.
9. When we are unable to control the relationship with a partner, we transfer our need to control to other people.
10. We are unable to stay at a job for long periods of time because of anxiety, or we refuse to let our partner work because we cannot be there to monitor her.
11. When we do not receive the attention that we want from a partner or other loved ones, we fall into a state of depression.
12. We suffer from stress-related gastrointestinal problems. These may include ulcers, esophageal reflux, constipation, diarrhea, or general stomach upset. We may also suffer from chronic stress-related headaches or backaches.
13. When a partner or loved one tells us that we are being controlling, we refuse to listen and insist that our behavior is normal. *We hear what we want to hear.*
14. We use sex as a tool of control and manipulation.
15. We stay in emotionally and/or physically abusive relationships, believing that we can fix a partner and somehow control his behavior.

Let's examine Nancy's past and relate it to her present. Several weeks prior to Nancy's visit at my apartment, she had telephoned me for support after a nasty argument with her husband regarding his whereabouts. During that conversation, I asked Nancy questions about her childhood and her relational history with men. The information she revealed to me then first made me suspect that she is a person who confuses love with obsession.

She told me that her parents were alcoholics who worked during the day and drank heavily at night. They argued often, and these angry words would sometimes escalate into physical violence. During particularly nasty fights, her father would storm out of the house and disappear for days at a time. When this happened, Nancy remembered feeling confused, abandoned, and alone. In fact, she recalled that these feelings overwhelmed her, causing her to become depressed and unattached to her world.

She went on to explain that at eighteen, she dated a marine named David who was emotionally unavailable and extremely abusive. She looked past his temper, however, believing that if she showed him enough love, she could somehow change his angry ways and thereby control the uncontrollable. So each time she was mistreated, she showed David that much more love. Their relationship abruptly ended in just two short months when she was hospitalized after David broke her arm and bruised her ribs. She reported that she would have stayed with him, despite his abuse, had her father not insisted on the breakup. She recalled becoming depressed for several months after their separation, totally drained of energy and unable to function. Sometime later she met Ron and "knew," as she put it, that she wanted to be with him forever.

Nancy's childhood was marked with parental alcoholism and violence, leaving her feeling neglected, alone, and confused. When her father disappeared for days at a time, she experienced deep feelings of abandonment that, unbeknownst to her, would stay with her into adulthood. Thus during the early part of her life, the first storm clouds of destruction appeared on the horizon. The storm would eventually grow into a powerful and uncontrollable force, ultimately obliterating every meaningful relationship she was in and leaving her emotionally devastated. The fuel for the storm, as with most people who confuse love with obsession, was overwhelming fear—fear of abandonment wrapped in distrust. She lived in a world of constant fear, believing that the men in her life would eventually leave her, just as her father had left her as a child. In her adulthood, she mistakenly believed that she could prevent relational collapses through controlling behaviors. What Nancy did not realize is that the more she tightened her grip, the more her suitors felt trapped. That she had managed to stay in a relationship with Ron for twelve years was a miracle, given some of her behaviors in the marriage. To be sure, Ron's behavior during their relationship was inexcusable and selfish. He is not, though, totally to blame for what happened. Nancy's obsessive need to control him caused him to feel trapped. Although I could not be sure, I suspected the only reason Ron had stayed with her for so long was out of concern for their children. I also suspected that it was no coincidence that the boys moved in with his parents. The entire family had grown tired of Nancy's obsessive ways and wanted out.

So what happened to Nancy? Months after her visit to my apartment, she informed me that Ron had filed for divorce and had moved with Denise to another city. The children were still living with Ron's parents and custody was being negotiated. She also told me that, through the help of her therapist, she was beginning to understand how her childhood and life experiences had contributed to her current predicament. More important, she said that she was learning to love herself with the help and support of others.

When we confuse love with obsession, we have a type of addiction that I have termed *relational dependency,* or *RD.* For our purposes, we can define RD as becoming grossly preoccupied with another person to the point of significantly impairing the ability to perform daily functions, including work, school, and child rearing. This is coupled with strong feelings of denial and, ultimately, a total loss of control. In fact, it is an insidious and cruel addiction that is often misunderstood and widely undetected. It takes a lifetime to become a person who is relationally dependent, and it is a problem that does not get better over time without help.

In the remaining pages of this book, we will look at the experiences of people who confuse love with obsession in detail. We will examine why we need to control, the various tools we use to keep control, and the misguided belief systems that keep us trapped in unhealthy partnerships. We will also examine how the cycle of control repeats itself and how the partner being controlled is emotionally and sometimes physically affected. Finally, we will discuss how to find a path to recovery. Here is an expanded version of the traits, characteristics, and behaviors of a person who confuses love with obsession. Do any of these strike a chord of familiarity?

1. We were emotionally abandoned and may have been verbally, psychologically, or physically abused (or all three) during childhood.

Being emotionally abandoned in conjunction with being verbally, psychologically, or physically abused is perhaps the primary causal factor for those of us who confuse love with obsession.

Growing up in a home where parents are constantly fighting leaves little time for the nurturing and support that a child needs for healthy emotional development. Those of us who grew up in this kind of environment were left feeling abandoned, alone, and confused. As a result, later in life we cling to any attention we might receive, even if this attention is unhealthy. If we have grown up in an environment where our parents were emotionally unavailable or were physically abusive, we seek attention from other sources and use control tactics to keep people from leaving us.

In the childhood homes of those of us who went on to confuse love with obsession, the following may have occurred:

- Abusive words and expressions from parents, including "You are worthless" and "You will never amount to anything." The most devastating: "I wish you were never born."
- Physical abuse, including unnecessary hard slapping, punching, and beatings as a result of misplaced rage by one or both parents. Children who are sexually molested also fall under this category (although the damage is also psychological).
- Psychological torture, including being forced to helplessly watch a sibling being beaten by a parent. Psychological torture can also include watching one parent hit the other parent.
- Parental addiction to alcohol and/or other drugs. Children who live under these circumstances grow up with the daily pain of a parent (or parents) who is caught up in the throes of a powerful chemical and psychological addiction. Parents who are drunk or strung out on drugs are emotionally and physically unavailable to their children, who subsequently feel unwanted and abandoned.
- Parents avoiding one another; this includes periods when

parents ignore each other and use the children as a pawn for attention. "She's my child. Don't go near her!" Another example would be one parent threatening the other with abandonment and kidnapping. "If you walk out that door, you will never see me or your daughter again!"

All of the above behaviors and actions are extremely damaging to a child's overall development and sense of self-esteem. Children who grow up in abusive homes often grow up to be abusers and to fear abandonment in their intimate relationships, which may explain the next characteristic.

2. We trap partners into relationships by withholding emotions or finances, or through other means of manipulation.

Afraid that people will suddenly leave us, we use emotions, finances, and other means of manipulation as a way of maintaining control over a partner. Manipulative behaviors may include, but are not limited to, the following:

- Withholding emotions from a partner, or punishing a partner by refusing to be supportive, loving, and giving. Our goal is to make him emotionally dependent on us. In reality, however, we are emotionally dependent on our partner.
- Withholding money from our partner, including cash and credit cards, because money represents freedom and, in our minds, a means for her to flee the relationship.
- Manipulating our partner into thinking he *has to* stay in the relationship. This means we manufacture serious problems and play the "guilt card." A statement such as, "Johnny needs you because he's having trouble in school," is an example of a manipulative statement.

3. We engage in acts of revenge against people we perceive as a threat to our relationships.

Our revenge can be against a partner or the people we perceive as a threat to our relationships. Our revenge takes the form of emotional, physical, or financial abuse. Examples of these behaviors include the following:

- Calling our partner names and obscenities in an attempt to bully him into making a confession of a suspected act of infidelity.
- Hitting our partner for an act or suspected act of infidelity, hoping to teach her that there are repercussions for "cheating." Some of us may have told our mate, "If I can't have you, nobody can," meaning that we beat our partner so she will look unattractive. This is a dangerous and sometimes fatal form of control.
- "Cutting off" a partner financially for alleged acts of infidelity by closing his bank accounts and credit cards so he does not have access to money. (Those of us who confuse love with obsession know a partner's credit card number by heart, in addition to his Social Security number.) The hope is to deny a partner the freedom to leave.
- Engaging in acts of revenge against those we perceive as a threat to our relationship; this may include slashing their tires, breaking their windows, making threatening phone calls, attempting to get them fired, or any intimidation that will cause harm or anxiety. Our number one goal is to drive a wedge between these persons and our partner, leading us to do almost anything to stop them from being together.

4. We are constantly preoccupied with our significant other's whereabouts, spending most of the day monitoring and tracking her physical and financial moves.

Because we are deeply afraid of being abandoned, we have an uncontrollable need to know the exact whereabouts of our partner. This causes us to do things such as the following:

- Following a partner to and from work and other places.
- Hiring a private detective to track a partner or install hidden surveillance equipment in our home. These devices may include cameras and recording devices.
- Secretly obtaining (and memorizing) the pass-codes to a partner's voice mail, pager, and e-mail accounts and then checking the partner's electronic messages daily.
- Eavesdropping on a partner's telephone calls and using technology that monitors call activity such as caller ID. This invasion of telephone privacy also includes using features such as "last number dialed" to discover the last person he called. If a number does not seem appropriate, we will call it obsessively until we discover who it is. We also audit the monthly phone bill to check for "questionable" numbers.
- Meticulously tracking a partner's financial transactions by calling her credit card companies to discover the location, date, and nature of a partner's whereabouts. We may monitor ATM transactions in the same manner.
- Driven by a fear of infidelity, secretly going through a partner's personal belongings, including wallets, purses, briefcases, coats, pants, or anyplace we think he may be hiding "evidence."
- Reading a partner's personal mail and any other correspondence.

5. We restrict a partner's ability to communicate with and/or have friends.

We view a partner's personal friendships as a threat to our relationship. We approve or disapprove of the company that she keeps. Our actions may include the following:

- Demanding that a partner abandon friendships that predated the relationship.
- Guilting a partner into spending time with us, rather than his friends. "She's not your girlfriend, you know" is an example of such a control tactic.
- Punishing a partner by becoming emotionally or verbally abusive if she does spend time with a friend.

6. We use food as a way of keeping a partner overweight, hoping that he will appear unattractive and thus undesirable to others.

This is a tactic we use in hopes that other people will find our mate undesirable. Some of these controlling behaviors may include the following:

- Buying only fatty foods that have a high caloric content.
- Tricking a partner into eating fatty foods against her will by secretly adding unhealthy ingredients to the food we prepare.
- Sabotaging a partner's weight-loss efforts by attacking his self-esteem. For example, we might say, "You're always going to be fat, so why do you bother dieting?"
- Refusing to allow a partner to exercise.

7. We may be coaddicted to alcohol, other drugs, food, or sex.

As people who confuse love with obsession, we are relationally dependent. Because many addictions are interrelated and are biological and psychological in nature, it is not uncommon for some of us to be suffering from a coaddiction. This means, in addition to our relationship troubles, we may also

- be dependent on alcohol and/or drugs in order to medicate emotional pain

- habitually overeat because we believe it helps to fill an emotional void
- have sex with multiple, anonymous people as a means of self-validation and attention

8. Our worst fear is being abandoned, and we will do *anything* to stop a partner from leaving.

We constantly feel like our partner is going to leave, causing us to suffer anxiety and panic attacks. Our behaviors may include

- suffering from anxiety attacks when we cannot locate our partner
- making countless "check-calls" to see if our partner is at home or work
- waking up in the middle of the night to see if our partner is still in bed with us
- not being able to sleep alone or go to bed until our partner joins us
- needing to be in the same room with our partner so we can watch and control his actions

9. When we are unable to control the relationship with a partner, we transfer our need to control to other people.

Because we are frustrated with the inevitable loss of control over a partner, we look for other people to control, especially children, parents, and other family members. This involves a psychological defense process called *displacement,* which means we direct the emotions we have for one person toward another. Examples of displacement include

- demanding the same standards we expect of our partner from our children, parents, or other family members and friends

- becoming verbally abusive to others because of our loss of control over a loved one
- using physical violence against other people because we are angry at actions or suspected actions of a mate

10. We are unable to stay at a job for long periods of time because of anxiety, or we refuse to let our partner work because we cannot be there to monitor her.

This is a common characteristic for those of us who confuse love with obsession. Examples of this type of behavior include the following:

- Going from job to job because we are so obsessed with our partner's whereabouts that we are unable to stay focused on our work
- Getting fired from a job because we are constantly late or absent from work because we are too busy tracking a partner's actions
- Refusing to let a significant other work because we do not want him to be in social situations where he may meet someone new
- Picking and choosing where a partner is employed, giving our "stamp of approval" before she can begin the job

11. When we do not receive the attention that we want from a partner or other loved ones, we fall into a state of depression.

When we do not receive the attention we feel we deserve from a partner, we view it as a form of rejection and find ourselves falling into a deep state of depression. This drains us of energy and can restrict our ability to function. The only way to return to "normal" is for us to receive the attention we desire and be given assurances that our partner (or other loved ones) will not abandon us. We may also throw emotional fits and temper tantrums until we receive the attention that we crave.

12. **We suffer from stress-related gastrointestinal problems. These may include ulcers, esophageal reflux, constipation, diarrhea, or general stomach upset. We may also suffer from chronic stress-related headaches or backaches.**

Controlling other people requires a great deal of energy. This, in combination with our deeply held fear of abandonment, causes damage to our body. By suffering from constant anxiety or panic attacks, worrying ourselves into "knots," and neglecting our emotional and physical health, our body responds by excreting powerful acids that disrupt the natural flow of the digestive system. It is not uncommon for those of us who confuse love with obsession to suffer from stress-related ulcers, irritable bowel syndrome, or other gastrointestinal problems. Stress can also manifest itself in other ways that affect the central nervous system (CNS), causing headaches and sometimes crippling, unexplained back pain.

13. **When a partner or loved one tells us that we are being controlling, we refuse to listen and insist that our behavior is normal.** *We hear what we want to hear.*

Over the course of time, the person we love eventually lets us know that our extreme control tactics have become intolerable. Because the effort we have put into controlling other people is so singular in focus, it has prevented many of us from seeing things as they really are as opposed to the way we wish them to be. When we are told things such as, "You are trying to control every part of my life," we respond with denial and justification. Our responses may include the following:

- "You are the one doing the controlling—not me!"
- "You are just saying that so you can get what you want."
- "You really don't mean what you are saying."
- "You are *making* me act this way."

It is as if we cannot hear the spoken words from the other person. We argue with him until he says the things we want to hear, for example, "I guess you are right; I should have been seeing things from your point of view."

14. We use sex as a tool of control and manipulation.

This control tactic is particularly effective for the person who confuses love with obsession because it is inherently emotionally based. Using sex as a tool of control can include the following behaviors:

- Withholding sex from a partner in order to "make a point."
- Introducing third parties (three-ways) into a relationship for the purpose of making a partner "more interested."
- Having sex with other people as a way of "getting back" at a partner, with the hope of making her jealous.
- Comparing our sexual performance with our partner's former love interest as a way of "checking out the competition" through interrogation tactics. For example, we may insist our partner answer this question: "Who was hotter in bed—me or your last girlfriend?"

15. We stay in emotionally and/or physically abusive relationships, believing that we can fix a partner and somehow control his behavior.

We have a need to "fix" our partner's problems and, in many ways, become his "savior." Examples of this characteristic include the following:

- Enduring physical and/or emotional abuse, believing that a partner will one day see that she is "hurting you and the relationship"
- Staying in an abusive relationship and believing that "If I show enough love, he will see how destructive his behavior is"
- Confusing verbal abuse with love, believing that "You only hurt the ones you love; that's why he calls me those names, you know"
- Confusing physical abuse with love, believing that "When he hits me, at least I know he cares"

So now our journey begins. The following pages will acquaint you with others, perhaps like yourself, who pathologically confuse love with obsession. Take note of their experiences and recognize any patterns that might fit your own personal situation. The last chapter of this book is dedicated to recovery, with resources you can use to transform your life. As I alluded to in the introduction, an addiction to another person is like a violent storm, causing great pain for everyone involved. However, *it doesn't have to be this way.* My hope for you is that you find that special place, somewhere between hope and fear, where storm clouds collide and the once destructive raindrops transform into gentle mists of harmony. Let's find that place together.

2

TOO MUCH
OF A GOOD THING

Desperately he tried to rush after her and follow her down,
but he was not allowed. The gods would not consent
to his entering the world of the dead a second time,
while he was still alive. He was forced to return
to the earth alone, in utter desolation.

—Ovid, *The Metamorphoses*

ROUGH TURBULENCE had made a freshly poured cup of coffee tip over on my tray table as the commercial passenger jet struggled to climb through a summer thunderstorm. We had been in the air only twenty-five minutes, and I was desperately wishing my flight from Chicago to Los Angeles would end. As hot liquid flowed ominously toward my legs, Chris, my flying partner, began frantically waving napkins in the air.

"Wipe it up quickly or it will burn you," he said. "Trust me, it hurts." But his next words were shocking.

"I know what it is like to be burned." He laughed nervously. "Trust me, it's no fun." Then he laughed again and added, "I have my dad to thank for that."

He became silent as he took it upon himself to wipe up the mess. Medium build, with short brown hair and emerald green eyes, at twenty-four years old he was indeed handsome. He continued blotting away at the coffee until it was no longer visible.

I first met Chris when he joined the support group I attended for the relationally addicted. He was a convicted stalker. That he was allowed to board the aircraft that day was a miracle, given his recent past. A year earlier, he had worked out a plea bargain for criminal trespassing and was sentenced to two years of probation with strict orders from the judge to seek counseling. He had to gain special permission from the Cook County Department of Corrections to leave Illinois, with the condition that he check in with his probation officer on a daily basis. The reason for his jaunt to California was therapeutic in nature, his counselor believing that the trip might allow him the opportunity to examine his past behaviors and perhaps find some time for self-discovery. When he offered me the free ticket out west as part of a buy-one-get-one-free sales promotion, I decided to accept. After we landed, he was heading up to the northern part of the state to do some sightseeing, and I was heading south, to San Diego, for a little R & R.

Through bits and pieces of information that he shared during group support meetings, I learned that he had grown up with a physically abusive father who would fly into drunken rages and then take out his frustrations on Chris and his family. Whenever a child grows up in this kind of caustic environment, whether the abuse is inflicted by a parent, sibling, or other caretaker, there is usually a direct effect on the way the child behaves later in life. The abuse can lead to a need to cling to and control others, a fear of rejection, a propensity to use violence, or the need to seek out revenge. Indeed, the primary causal factor for people who go on to confuse love with obsession can be traced back to traumatic childhoods.

I strongly believed that Chris's upbringing had influenced the way he related to women, and his comment about "having his father to thank" made me curious, and so I asked, "Your father burned you?"

As Chris considered the question, the aircraft leveled off to its assigned cruising altitude, and the turbulence gave way to a smoother ride. Moments later, against the quiet hum of the jet's engines, he began to offer some details.

Chris had one brother, two years his elder, and had grown up on Chicago's South Side in a modest home. "Oh, my father was a complete jerk. One Saturday morning, after he had been boozing all night, I found myself on the receiving end of a hot cup of coffee. Apparently, he didn't like the fact that I had slept in late and had not yet gotten around to mowing the lawn." He shook his head. "He gave me third-degree burns on my arm. Do you want to see? The scar is still visible." Without waiting for my reply, he rolled up his right shirtsleeve halfway, revealing a small patch of tan, disfigured skin atop the forearm. "Not very pretty, is it?" I shook my head in disbelief and then prodded him for more details about his past.

He reported that when he was twelve years old, he watched his father stick a loaded revolver in his mother's mouth, threatening to pull the trigger if she did not "shut up" during a heated argument about family finances. Apparently, this was the way his father would make demands on his family, through intimidation and acts of violence.

He continued talking: "My dad went out of his way to put me down, calling me names like 'loser' and 'worthless bastard.' No matter what I did to try to impress him or to live up to his expectations, it was never good enough." Chris pressed the button on the side of his armrest to recline his seat. "So Dad used to get *really* drunk, then *really* angry. Sometimes, without reason, he would come into our bedroom in the middle of the night, flip on the light switch, and tell me and my brother to 'shuck 'em,' meaning that we were to pull down our pants and lie down flat on the bed while he used a hard leather belt to beat us." He lowered his head. "The bastard only felt satisfied when he saw welts forming. I eventually became immune to the pain." He said this with a flash of anger in his voice.

"The one thing that always got to me was watching Dad pummel away at my brother. You see, 'dear old Dad' would force me to watch as he beat my brother to a pulp. I can still see the expression of horror on my brother's face as my dad repeatedly struck him." He inhaled deeply. "That was worse than when Dad would use the belt on me." He raised his head. "Nobody deserves to be put through that kind of abuse."

Chris paused to reflect, slowly using his index finger to trace around the rim of a can of cola. "Mom would just sit in her bedroom when Dad beat us, turning up the volume on the TV and then use her hands to cover her ears. She never intervened or tried to stop him—not even once. In time, my brother and I gave up on thinking that she would come to our rescue and stop him. I remember that when our teachers used to call the house and ask Mom why our faces were black and blue, she would lie and say stuff like, 'They were playing football and things must have gotten out of hand—you know kids.'" He took a sip of soda and then examined the can in a reflective manner as he held it in front of him. "My dad even had her trained to make him drinks; she was just as bad as him."

Chris scratched the top of his head as if he were trying to remember something. "My counselor told me that what happened at home when I was a kid made me into the person I am today, you know—a freaking *stalker*." He laughed as he enunciated the word *stalker*, attempting to minimize the label. "I know now that I was trying to find the attention that I was not receiving at home through the girls that I attached myself to. I wish I would have seen the patterns before."

"Do you want to tell me about those patterns?" I asked.

A flight attendant came by and refreshed our drinks, allowing Chris time to think about the question.

"It all started with Stacy; she was my first 'love.' Oh man, I wanted to be with her in the worst way. Looking back on that relationship, I can see how I behaved like a total jerk." He another took another sip of cola. "You know—I met her because I was a kind of jock. Dad forced me onto the school wrestling team because he thought that sports would 'make a man out of me.' So being popular and all, I had no problems finding girls to mess around with."

It made perfect sense to me that Chris had become sexually active at such a young age. His parents did not make him feel valued at home, so he looked for validation through other means, namely girls. According to Chris, he would go from house to house and have his "pick" of girls who were willing to have sex with him. In time, the young Casanova's rounds brought him into contact with someone whom he liked more than the others.

"I'm not sure what made me latch on to her in the way I did, but I think it had something to do with the way she made me feel inside—like I mattered, you know? We used to spend *so* much time together. We'd talk all night on the telephone, hang out at her house, or sometimes just do nothing but still have fun." He smiled, then laughed. "And of course there was the sex—but I really wasn't into her for that. She eventually broke up with me because of what happened."

As he continued narrating the details of his relationship with Stacy, I began to see events from his past unfold like a motion picture in my mind. I could imagine Chris's father going into his usual drunken rages, calling Chris obscenities and then taking out his frustrations with his fists. To escape his dysfunctional home life, Chris would run to Stacy, feeling happy as she held him in her arms and secure in the knowledge that she cared. In time, he became hooked on her attention like a potent drug, seeking out her affection on a daily basis to the point that he could not separate himself from her.

"Stacy made me feel safe. I didn't have to worry about how I behaved in front of her or try to live up to her expectations. She listened to my problems and treated me with respect. I never got that at home from my parents. But I ruined our relationship because of my neediness."

Because time spent apart from Stacy made him feel empty inside, Chris found himself needing to increase his contact with her. He would call her dozens of times each day and then, late at night, appear at her house unannounced and bang on the door, asking her to come outside to talk. When she would walk to school with her girlfriends, she would see Chris running up the street with his hands waving in the air, calling out her name and asking her to wait so that he could join her. When her last class of the day concluded, she would find him standing outside in the school yard, waiting to walk her home. In time, Chris's face would greet her around every corner she turned and every door that she walked though. Soon, she started to recoil at the sight of him.

"She said that she felt trapped and wanted 'space' because we were spending way too much time together. It drove a stake through my heart because I thought she liked being with me."

Chris had already decided in his mind that they were meant to be together, regardless of Stacy's wishes. Her request for more space translated into her deception in Chris's mind, and he believed that she had found someone new. Unfounded thoughts of her betrayal began to swirl in his head, and he became increasingly anxious during the hours they were apart. He began to obsessively "check-call" her home on an hourly basis, even as late as two o'clock in the morning, just to make sure that she was home. When her parents would take the phone off the hook, he would become frustrated, cornering her the next day at school and angrily interrogating her. The more time he had to think about Stacy and their collapsing relationship, the more anxious and paranoid he became. It was only a matter of time before he started stalking her and, ultimately, becoming violent.

Chris continued, "I was hiding in the bushes one day after school to see what she was up to. Stacy was talking to another boy from the neighborhood, and it got me pissed. After she left the scene, I picked up a discarded beer bottle and used it on the other guy's head. I was told he had to be taken to the emergency room to get a bunch of stitches in his forehead. When Stacy and her parents caught word of what I had done from people in the neighborhood, they decided to sever the relationship and cut me out of her life.

"For months I would call her house and plead with Stacy to take me back, sometimes threatening suicide. When her parents demanded that I stop calling, I'd show up outside of their home and sulk on the sidewalk for hours. Other times, I would climb the fence of their backyard and peek inside of her bedroom window to see if she was there with another guy. It was all so bizarre, you know? Well, it was all forced to an end one night when the cops caught me spray painting the word *bitch* on her garage. Luckily, her parents dropped the charges. Eventually Stacy and her family moved to another city, when her dad got transferred with his job."

Had Chris been reared in an environment where his parents had given him the love and attention he needed as a child, he might not have clung to Stacy in such an obsessive way.

Chris's father was too absorbed in his drinking and abusive outbursts to have bothered with tending to his children's needs, and Chris's mother was too busy acting as the enabler. As he had mentioned, no matter how hard he tried to gain his father's approval, nothing worked. And so as Chris got older, he continued his pattern of seeking out validation and affection through the women he encountered, treating them possessively and obsessing over their every move.

Chris continued talking about his patterns. "So after Stacy, I dated other girls—but all of them dumped me because they wanted 'space.' Sometimes I would get really pissed off at them when they wanted to break it off." He paused briefly, shrugged his shoulders, and shook his head. "So I'd go by their house and throw a rock through their window or take a nail and run it alongside of their car. I got caught a few times, and my dad would have to come bail me out of jail. I can remember on the car ride home, he would say, 'You are such a freak. I wish you were never born.' Well I know now that I did these things because I felt rejected and wanted revenge." Chris looked down at his tray table. "But nothing compares to what happened last year." He shook his head slowly while struggling with difficult memories. "I totally lost control."

Chris went on to report that when he was twenty-three, he moved into the city and took a job as a mailroom clerk at a downtown office supply company and soon crossed paths with a nursing student named Brenda. She was employed as a part-time server at a popular coffee café and at twenty-five was extremely goal oriented. They had met innocently enough when Chris saw her through the window of the café on his way to work and became immediately captivated by her gentle beauty. It wasn't long before he started inventing reasons to talk to her, popping into the café throughout the day and inquiring about the different exotic blends. Eventually, he worked up enough courage to ask her out for dinner, and as time continued, they began to date exclusively.

Very early in their relationship during a leisurely evening walk, Brenda told Chris that she had "never met a man quite like him before." Unbeknownst to her, Brenda's comment would become all that he needed to hear to become instantly addicted to her and their relationship. Soon, every sentence that departed his lips started off with *Brenda,* and he could not chase the image of her smiling face out of his mind. And while the sex they shared was passionate, it was the affection she showed him that often sent him into a drunken, giddy state of euphoria.

But in time, his past would become his present, and the obsessive ways in which he related to women began to surface once again.

"For the first time in my life, I truly felt wanted and loved. Being with her made me feel complete. I mean, I honestly felt like when we were together, anything was possible. I cannot describe in words to you how good it felt knowing that I had found someone who *wanted* to be with me. But I didn't want her to know this or she might start asking for 'space' like all of the other women in my life. So I figured that I could make her want me more by giving the impression that I was dis-interested. When she would telephone, I would purposely let her calls go to voice mail and later tell her that 'I was out with friends.' Although she didn't know it, I never left the house. You see—I was too afraid that I might miss her call."

As their relationship continued, Chris became more ob-sessive. He began showering her with unexpected gifts such as jewelry and expensive clothes, things that he could ill-afford to buy, but nonetheless purchased, hoping to show her love through acts of kindness. He sent her a vase of roses each week at the café and romantic letters in the mail to her home.

Chris would write about his fantasies of their life together, with predictions of good times ahead. Although bemused by his behavior, Brenda chalked it up to his eccentric personality and continued focusing on her future.

Eventually, goal-oriented Brenda, who still lived at home with her parents, began a nursing internship at a downtown hospital. The schedule was extremely demanding, often requiring her to be at the hospital for long periods at a time with only a few hours off between shifts. After work, she would come home exhausted and head straight to bed. Despite knowing of her need to rest, Chris would call her anyway, needing what had become his daily dose of affection. When this happened, Brenda's protective mother would tell him to call back later, explaining that Brenda was asleep and needed her rest. But Chris could not accept her request, feeling emotionally neglected and at times irritated. In time he began to believe that Brenda was purposely avoiding him, and his mind would then begin to race, as it had many times before in his life, with unfounded thoughts of infidelity. It was then that he began to cyber-stalk her.

He quickly continued. "One night when we finally did get the chance to spend time together, I secretly went through her purse and wrote down her credit card, Social Security, and ATM numbers. I figured that if I couldn't be with her, I could at least find out what the hell she was doing. It was easy enough; all I had to do was go on the Internet and visit the Web sites she had her accounts with. I could then punch in her numbers and have instant access to her life. From the information I was able to obtain from her financial transactions, I could then look for any spending patterns. If I saw that she was frequenting certain places after work, it was a simple matter of parking outside of the establishment and watching her with my binoculars. I never caught her doing anything though," recalled Chris, who would spend hours on the Internet to track Brenda's every move. But this was not the only way he would monitor Brenda.

He went on to report that he would surreptitiously ransack through her purse, coat pockets, and pants, searching for anything that might lend evidence to his misguided feelings of betrayal. When he could not find the answers he was looking for, he would record the phone numbers of males he had discovered in her address book and investigate their backgrounds online. Sometimes he would even call them, pretending to be an "old friend of Brenda's" and investigate the nature of their association. "Hello, this is Dan, a friend of Brenda's. She asked me to call you to see if you can make it to a party on Friday night; you two are dating again now, right?" mimicked Chris in an altered voice, attempting to show me how he was able to manipulate others into providing him information.

But soon, Chris's delicate house of cards, glued together with lies, deception, and manipulation, began to collapse as he became immersed in his obsession over her.

"Things went from bad to worse when I started calling up her job and demanding to speak to her. When her co-workers told me that she was unavailable, I would question them and ask where she was. Other times, I would get really anxious and just show up at the hospital and drive around the parking lot, searching for her red hatchback. On more than one occasion, I actually went into the hospital cafeteria and waited to catch her on break, just to spend time with her. And of course there were the drive-bys. That's when I would circle around her home all night to make sure she had her car parked in the driveway. If I saw an unfamiliar vehicle parked in front of her house, I would wait for hours to find out who it was. Usually, though, it was a friend of the family or a relative. You know, I missed a lot of work during that time period because of my addiction. I am beginning to learn through counseling that it was part of my entire pattern."

Eventually, Chris's stalking activities began to catch up with him. It would be only a matter of time before Brenda discovered that the man she thought she knew was a total stranger.

He continued his story, "So that's when I got busted and she started pulling back. One night she called me and said that she was pissed that I had been going through her bank accounts. Pretending to be shocked, I asked her to explain. She mentioned having received a telephone call from her bank's security department and that 'red flags' were going up everywhere because of multiple log-ons to her account. Of course I denied it, but I knew she wasn't buying it."

Chris went on to report that his life began to spiral out of control. He was only working two or three days a week, reducing his schedule and telling his employer that it was due to family problems. In reality, he was not able to focus on work because he had become exhausted from his late-night stalking adventures. His obsession with Brenda had become his new full-time job. He was also experiencing powerful panic attacks, coupled with extreme anxiety.

Chris explained his anxiety: "Being with Brenda was kind of like being addicted to a drug. When I was not with her or following her, I would experience withdrawal. My body would shake and I would freak out. There was no way I could stay at work at that point because I couldn't concentrate on my job."

Chris's perceptions about withdrawal were right on target. He had become so emotionally caught up with Brenda and the energy he put into stalking her that his relationship with her had become the sole driving force behind his every action. In order to feel "normal" again, he had to be with her. The fact that he had a job with responsibilities was of little consequence.

For Brenda the last straw came when she discovered that messages on her answering machine had been mysteriously erased. Chris had obtained the machine's pass-code and was relentlessly calling each day to monitor and delete messages. After putting together all of the bizarre incidents in her life, including the deleted messages, complaints from co-workers of a "strange man lurking around in the parking lot," and the recent telephone call from her bank, she decided to pull the plug on the relationship.

"Chris, I know what you have been doing, and I don't want to see you anymore. Do not call me at home or work, come by my house, or buy me any gifts. If you don't do as I ask, I am going to get a restraining order against you," mimicked Chris, repeating the message that Brenda had left for him on his answering machine informing him of the breakup.

This decision would prove to be a terrible miscalculation on her part, however, as she had no idea that Chris was incapable of accepting her wishes.

"I just wanted to talk to her—to tell her that I was sorry," recalled Chris, who had refused to understand that Brenda wanted out. "I ended up going to the hospital after she left that message on my machine—but when I tried to talk to her, she called security on me," Chris said.

The situation came to a head the next night. According to Chris, "I think around two or three in the morning, I drove by her house with my headlights turned off. I could see that one of the windows was slightly ajar because the drapes were blowing in the wind. I parked the car down the street and walked up to the house, somehow getting the courage to open the window and crawl through. I tiptoed into her bedroom and stared over her beautiful body while she slept in the moonlight. If it weren't for her stupid dog, I might have been able to gently awaken her with a kiss and then tell her how sorry I was about everything." Chris's eyes opened wide as he explained how his Prince Charming fairy tale morphed into a nightmare. "But the dog's barking caused everyone in the house to get up, including Brenda. She started screaming. I tried to cover her mouth so she wouldn't wake up the whole neighborhood, but it was too late. Her dad came rushing out of nowhere and jumped on my back. We got into a scuffle, and I don't remember much after that, except that I hit him with a ceramic lamp. Before I knew what was happening, I found myself in handcuffs and was being carted off by Chicago's finest to police headquarters."

He explained what happened next, this time in the court-room surrounded by Brenda and her family. "The judge told me not to go anywhere near her home or work or in any way come into contact with her. He even called me a stalker. Now I am on probation for two years."

Indeed, Chris's experience that day in the court was the catalyst he needed to jolt him onto a path of recovery. After his conviction, Chris began the courageous process of attending a support group for the relationally addicted, coupled with weekly therapy sessions. I knew that newcomers, such as Chris, did not walk into these groups casually. They end up coming to such a gathering because something horrible occurred in their lives, often with devastating results. Addicts call this experience "bottoming out." It represents a critical turning point for someone confronting the reality that his destructive behaviors are no longer controllable. Bottoming-out experiences commonly include the loss of a job; being expelled from the lives of family, friends, and other loved ones; or financial desolation. Bottoming-out experiences may also include being arrested, inflicting physical harm against a loved one (or others), suicide attempts, or homelessness. When this "aha" moment occurs, an inner voice (perhaps the voice of God) says, "Something has to change, or you will be destroyed." Thankfully for Chris, he recognized his inner voice in the courtroom that fateful day.

"After I was convicted," Chris continued, "I began to see what a mess my life had become. Every relationship I had been in with a woman had turned out to be a disaster. I got so hooked on their attention that I would do anything to keep getting it from them. As a kid, my parents weren't able to emotionally care for me, so I looked for others to provide that for me.

"My obsessive behaviors include forcing myself on others and trying to make them love me. It's part of what I am working on in counseling. It's not an easy task, but I am trying."

Because the blueprint of how we give and receive love is learned from the relationships with our parents, we interact with others later in life in ways that are similar. As a child, he sought his abusive father's approval (or affection) but never received it, and he expected his mother's intervention during times his father would beat him but was ignored and, in the process, betrayed. In Chris's quest for love with the women he encountered, he repeated the relationship with his father by obsessively seeking a woman's affection. When he perceived that they were not giving him the love he tried so hard to win, he would assign the causal reason as betrayal, unconsciously tracing back to the feelings of betrayal he had for his mother.

Whenever a woman would pull back from Chris because of his obsessive behaviors, he would become anxious and begin to stalk her, gaining closeness with the object of his affection and the fantasy of reconciliation. Quite simply, the more women pushed him away, the more he was drawn closer to them. What else could he do? He had learned as a child that rejection was part of the love game, causing him to fight that much harder to win the prize of affection.

He concluded his tale, "I know now that I have a real problem—a sickness. With the help of my counselor, and of course the support group, I am hoping to put my life back together again. My goal is to one day learn how to love myself, and with any luck, to learn how to love someone else. It's going to take awhile, however."

Stalking *can* (but not always does) become an integral part of relational dependency. Stalkers may spend entire days obsessing over the object of their affection, losing their sense of reality and, in time, losing themselves. In Chris's situation, his obsessive behaviors can be traced to the emotional damage he received as a youth, when paternal abuse caused extreme feelings of low self-esteem and, in many ways, self-hatred. The fact that he became quickly and emotionally dependent upon the women he encountered demonstrates the lack of love that he had for himself. In his subconscious mind, the women he latched on to acted as a kind of knight in shining armor. He believed that they had come galloping into his life to rescue him from his overwhelming feelings of low self-esteem and loneliness. In his attempts to ingratiate himself with these women and his constant need to be reassured about their level of commitment to the relationship, he became overbearing and only served to drive them away. Chris can be classified as a *rejected stalker*, according to Paul Mullen from the Victorian Institute of Forensic Mental Health.* Specifically, rejected stalkers use stalking as a way of substitut-

---

* Paul E. Mullen, Michele Pathé, and Rosemary Purcell, "The Management of Stalkers," *Advances in Psychiatric Treatment*, no. 7 (2001): 335–42, apt.rcpsych.org/cgi/content/full/7/5/335.

ing for the lost relationship. For Chris, the more he sensed that Brenda was trying to avoid him, the more anxious and paranoid he became. The more he stalked her, the more addicted he became to their relationship. The culmination of his obsessive ways caused him to lash out uncontrollably, which ultimately led to his breaking into her home and assaulting her father.

When stalking is part of relational dependency, some or all of the following beliefs, behaviors, and characteristics are usually present:

- We feel an instant and immediate attachment to another person. We find ourselves asking, "How can I *make* this person love me?" rather then asking, "How do I really feel about this person?"
- We have wild, unrealistic fantasies about the object of our affection. We think, "How can I get this person to share her life with me?" rather then wondering "How can we create a life together?"
- We have an inability to view the person as an individual. We refer to the relationship (or fantasy of the relationship) in the plural rather than the singular, for example, using "we" rather than "I" during conversations.
- We make scores of telephone calls to a partner's home or workplace (or both) each day, hoping to speak with the person or discover his location.
- We vocally impersonate friends or family members of the object of our affection to obtain information.
- We obsessively buy unwanted gifts, such as candy, jewelry, or clothes, hoping to obtain love through acts of kindness.
- We obsessively send letters, cards, e-mails, or faxes to a partner, believing this is an appropriate form of showing affection.

- We use the Internet to cyber-stalk, using deceptively obtained personal information (bank or credit card numbers) to investigate, monitor, and track spending or travel patterns.
- We become enraged with misguided feelings of jealousy and seek revenge, which may include the destruction of personal property or acts of physical violence.
- We physically stalk the object of our obsession, watching where a partner goes, with whom she interacts, and how she relates to others.

Because many of us, like Chris, did not feel valued as children, we have learned to look for validation through our adult relationships with others. We then come to depend on a relationship to fill the emptiness left by a lack of self-love. When our partner cannot or does not meet our emotional needs, we attempt to take control. We come to believe that being in a relationship means being in control of another person. We forsake and abandon relationships with those who once held importance in our lives and instead focus all of our energy on the current object of our obsession. When someone threatens our sense of security with the person we love, we become angry, paranoid, and anxious. Fueled by fear, we act out in ways that ultimately destroy that which we so desperately wish to preserve—*ourselves.* Throughout the whole painful process, we lose our identity in a powerful vortex of obsession. We are so busy trying to manipulate the other person into loving us that we neglect the most important relationship of all—*the relationship with ourselves.* The journey toward the path of healing can only begin when we recognize how our destructive patterns in the pursuit of love take us to the depths of pain.

Imagine Chris as a tightrope walker, learning his trade as a child without encouragement or support from his teachers and yet still being able to find balance on the wire. As time went on and he grew older, he learned to perfect his walk, becoming encouraged by cheers in the crowd and drawing energy from the people's attention—ever so carefully, balancing, walking, balancing . . .

Then one day he realized that in order to keep his admirers impressed, and in order to keep drawing energy from them, he had to learn new and more dangerous tricks. So he continued precariously tiptoeing on the wire, becoming increasingly emboldened by their attention—ever so carefully, balancing, walking, balancing . . .

But in time his new tricks became old, and the crowds began to dissipate. Not knowing how to create new material, he continued walking the wire, performing his old acrobatic feats of wonder and eventually becoming complacent. Suddenly, during one of the routines that he had done a hundred times before, he loses his balance and falls to the ground.

Chris knew that his dangerous walk on the tightrope would eventually lead to his undoing. But what else could he do? The game of balancing on the wire and gaining energy from the crowds brought him too much joy. In the end, he decided that the danger to him was more than a fair price to pay for what he considered to be the walk of *love.*

SOMETIMES, MONEY DOES BUY YOU LOVE

O ruler of the gods, if I have deserved this treatment,
and it is your will that I perish with fire, why withhold
your thunderbolts? Let me at least fall by your hand.
Is this the reward of my fertility, of my obedient service?

—Thomas Bulfinch, *The Age of Fable*

"I'LL TAKE CARE OF THE RENT THIS MONTH. Save your money and don't stress yourself out."

"I can buy that for you—it's not that much."

"Let me take care of that bill for you. I know you are trying."

"Don't think of it as my money—it's *our* money. What's mine is yours."

On the surface, statements like these appear genuine, caring, and perhaps even sincere, right? However, appearances can be deceiving, especially when dealing with a love addiction. What role does money play in relationships for those of us who confuse love with obsession? Do we as relationally addicted people unintentionally attract mates who are financially needy? And why do we have an overwhelming need to provide for a partner's monetary needs while neglecting our own? Is there something in our past that would make us want to assume the role of caretaker and then use that role to control our partner?

With the knowledge from the previous chapters, we now realize that past childhood experiences, which are deeply rooted in the psyche, have a direct impact on how we relate to and interact with our partner. To outsiders, some of the roles we adopt may appear noble, even "saviorlike." This happens when others believe that we are selflessly attending to our partner's needs, while purposefully neglecting our own. What outsiders don't realize is that our "good deeds," which often include financial support, are nothing more than an extension of our pathological need to control our partner. In short, some relationally obsessed people use money as a way of trapping their mate into a relationship, disguising their outwardly noble efforts in the name of "love."

The old cliché "Money can't buy you love" isn't necessarily true for those of us who confuse love with obsession. For the relationally obsessed, what money does buy is the *illusion* of love and in many instances, the *lie* of love. Because many of us grew up in fluid environments, where home life and parental relationships were anything but secure, we may have unintentionally found ourselves in the role of caretaker. In Robin Norwood's best-selling book, *Woman Who Love Too Much: When You Keep Wishing and Hoping He'll Change,* she exposed this problem in copious detail. Using money to keep another attached to the relationship is a form of excessive caretaking.

Almost all of us who confuse love with obsession experience a terrifying, almost paralyzing, fear of abandonment. Because we live with the daily torture of worrying whether a partner will leave us, we create built-in safeguards to assure that being alone (or abandoned) does not become a reality. There is nothing more assuring to the addict than knowing we have an "ace in the hole" when exerting control over our partner, and trying to make a partner feel she needs the relationship for financial reasons is one of the more potent hands in our deck of cards.

In many ways, we regress to childlike behaviors when using money as a means of controlling our partner. This can be likened to a ten-year-old who, after buying candy at the dime store, offers his treasures to the neighborhood children in order to gain their acceptance and attention. To keep his newfound friends, however, he quickly learns that he must have a constant supply of sweets. And the same can be said of a child who desires the latest, greatest toy, hoping to buy the affection of her friends.

An example of how money can be used as a tool of control in addictive relationships can been witnessed in the case of Patrick, a young man whom I met at the gym and occasionally "spotted" when he lifted weights. He and I spoke with one another at least three times a week, eventually bonding because of our mutual admiration for free weights. From talking to him, I learned that he worked at an accounting firm as a computer specialist. I also observed that he never *ever* missed a workout and meticulously attended to his appearance in an almost obsessive way.

During a particularly slow October evening at the gym, Patrick approached me and asked for assistance at the flat bench. He was wearing his normal gym outfit: cutoff navy blue sweatpants, a gray tank top that exposed a hairy, chiseled chest, and brown, cross-trainer-type sneakers. I often wondered if he wore these clothes to "show off" his massive physique. Indeed, at twenty-nine years old, Patrick was a walking fitness centerfold, his muscles finely sculptured, with a perfectly shaped torso that was complemented by pair of well-developed legs. In fact, whenever he walked by, most of the women at the gym would swing their heads around in admiration. I knew, however, that his buff look was, in part, artificial, given that weeks before, he had admitted to me that he was using steroids, spending hundreds of dollars each month on injections. He even confided in me that the price of the drugs had made him go in debt.

As the sound of classic rock played loudly in the background, Patrick began loading two, forty-five-pound plates on each side of the universal bar. He appeared somewhat unfocused, as if his mind were someplace else. His normal "killer smile" was missing as well, replaced with a more serious, frustrated look. After he finished loading the weights, he said in a low voice, "I'm *really* angry today, so I am lifting a little more than I usually do." He felt the black stubble of one day's growth on his face as he considered the amount of weight on the bar. "Yep, I think I can handle this amount." He proceeded to lie down on the bench in preparation for his chest workout.

Concerned about his comment, I decided to find out what was troubling him and asked for details.

Moments later, after pumping out a set of ten clean repetitions, he started to talk. "It's my wife, Sarah. We've only been married five years, and I think she is getting ready to split." He placed his hands on the lifting bar. "She told me this morning that she was tired of my 'control tactics' and that if she had the cash, she would have already left me." He tightened his grip on the bar and looked at me with a stone-cold face. "She's acting like an ungrateful bitch. She actually told me that I made her feel 'trapped.' She ought to be thankful that I take care of her the way I do. How many women would *love* to be in a relationship with a guy who paid for everything." He said this with conviction in his voice, as if making a statement rather than asking a question. I allowed him to execute and finish his first set of repetitions on the bench before probing for more details.

"We've been married for five years, and she never gave me the impression that she was unhappy." He said this while sitting on the edge of the bench and looking directly at me. "Anything that Sarah wants, she gets. I pay for everything you know."

Patrick went on to explain Sarah's "terrific life," as he put it. She stayed home most of the day, cleaning the house and attending to other chores. She did not work because, as Patrick put it, "A woman's place is in the home." If she required money, she simply had to ask. *If* Patrick approved of the expense, he gave her the money. And he did, after all, in his self-described benevolence, give her a weekly allowance she could spend on whatever she desired. It wasn't a great deal of money but just enough for her to indulge herself, such as a trip to the beauty salon to get her hair styled. He also provided her with a car so that she could attend to household errands, something else that he considered "generous." The life he offered to Sarah through his so-called generosity was "more than any woman could want," to hear him tell it. According to Patrick, she was "free" to come and go as she pleased, shop where she wanted, and as long as she was home when he was done with the workday, there would be no problems. "She has it made. I am shocked that she would want to leave me," he reported.

Cracks in his utopian view of the life that he offered Sarah began to appear when he relayed to me that she had recently expressed a desire to attend school. "She got this crazy idea that she could become some sort of interior designer and go around telling people how to decorate their homes. There's no money in that. Plus, I don't especially like the idea of her meeting strangers—too many freaks out there. When she asked me for the money to pay for tuition, I told her flat out, 'NO!' It was for her own good and her own protection."

Although he tried to paint me a picture of care and concern for Sarah, I sensed that his true motivations were far
more self-serving. The fact that he believed she should stay
home during the day and not work, coupled with his refusal
to let her attend school, represented a more serious issue,
which I suspected was a deeply held fear of abandonment.
I was also beginning to suspect that there was more to his
near-obsessive need to appear "hulklike," especially after
learning that he used steroids. We finished with the chest exercises and made our way to the cardio room, getting onto
adjacent treadmills where we could continue our conversation. I wanted to know more about why Patrick refused to let
his wife work or attend school. More important, I wanted to
discover if something had happened in his past that made him
behave so macholike in the present.

"So what about this a-woman's-place-is-in-the-home
comment that you made? Tell me, why do you believe this?" I
said, trying to present my questions in a nonconfrontational
manner, purposefully focusing my attention on the control
buttons of the treadmill and adjusting my speed to match
Patrick's slow and steady pace.

He took several minutes to consider my questions before
answering: "Well it's true, you know. If you give a woman too
much freedom, she'll eventually find someone else and dump
you. I've seen it many times before, including with my own
mother."

He went on to report that he was an only child who grew
up in a blue-collar neighborhood of Chicago where his
parents instilled in him the importance of family and hard
work. He characterized his home life as one that was happy
and loving, until something devastating occurred at the age
of twelve.

According to Patrick, "When I was a kid, my old man

worked ten-hour days at a steel mill." He turned his head in my direction. "During the day while he was at work, Mom worked at our parish, doing administrative work and light typing." He paused for a moment to wipe away a few beads of sweat from his forehead. "I mean, who would think you could get into trouble at a church? Anyway, my mom started having an affair with some guy who used to do handy work around the parish. Yeah, he was handy all right—handy at stealing people's mothers!" He shook his head and heavily exhaled through his nostrils. "Dad and I found out about it when she left us a note, telling us that she had decided to end the marriage and move in with *Ted*, her new love. Can you believe my parents were married for almost fifteen years— and then she goes and pulls some shit like that? Well, after Mom walked out on us, Dad was never the same. He got really depressed for a few months and emotionally shut down, staying in his room for hours at a time and sometimes missing work because he was so out of it. I spent a lot of time helping him get through what she had done to him. He cried so much. It's not easy for a kid to watch his father break down like that, man; it breaks your freaking heart.

"When she jetted on us like that, she left my dad and me to fend for ourselves. Instead of playing ball with my buddies after school, I was at home cleaning the house and doing the stuff Mom should have been there to do. My dad and I got real close, and things eventually got better with him. In time he finally snapped out of his depression, but the toll on his health was pretty bad. He had a heart attack last year, which I still think was partly caused by what my mom did to him years ago." He looked away momentarily and then looked at me again. "So you see, dude, that is the reason I don't play the 'trust game' with women. When they are at home, they stay out of trouble."

"And away from other men," he might just as well have concluded. Clearly, Patrick was carrying his painful childhood experience into his adult relationship with Sarah. In his confused mind, he had consciously linked women, marriage, and employment with infidelity. The difficult, traumatic memory of his mother's abandonment had left an indelible scar on his psyche. Hoping to avoid an agonizing postcard from the past in his marriage with Sarah, he used money as a way of controlling her, granting and denying her monetary wishes like an all-powerful, arrogant king. Keeping her financially dependent upon him guaranteed that she would not have the resources to leave. And his refusal to let her work or attend school furthered his grip of control by (1) limiting the people she came into contact with, thereby reducing the possibility of infidelity, and (2) controlling her knowledge base, which Patrick feared would allow her to gain the necessary skills to become marketable in the workplace and, ultimately, free of her dependence on him for money.

Based on Patrick's facial expressions and the tone of his voice when he spoke, I suspected that he might have experienced a twisted kind of high when considering his wife's financial requests, feeling a surge of power whenever she approached him for money. It made sense that he might feel this way, given the unresolved feelings of anger he had toward his mother after she abandoned him. By acting as caretaker for Sarah, he could control her while subconsciously exacting revenge against his mother.

What he was failing to realize, or refusing to see, was that his controlling behaviors were beginning to take a toll on Sarah and their marriage. The more he restricted her movements and controlled the "purse strings," the more Sarah resented him and their marriage. He was choking their marriage to death through his control tactics.

Before our time at the gym ended, I wanted Patrick to consider why his wife was feeling controlled and how his obsessive behaviors were damaging their relationship, so I said the following: "Don't get mad at me, Patrick, but I want to ask you something. How would you feel if someone told you that *you* could not work, *you* could not go to school, and *you* could not have any money unless someone granted you permission?" I asked this cautiously and with a soothing voice, concerned that his state of mind might cause him to become angrier.

Moments later, after taking time to mentally formulate an answer, he gave his response. "I wouldn't like it at all, to tell you the truth," he said, using an unexpected reflective voice. "I just don't want to lose her. I go to great lengths to try and make her feel cared for and loved. What else am I supposed to do?" he said, lowering his head slowly.

Because I suspected that he was trying to control Sarah in another way, I asked, "Is that why you work out as much as you do and take those steroids—because you want to appear attractive to Sarah so that she won't look at other men?"

He laughed nervously, giving the impression that his secret had been exposed. "Yes, it's true," he admitted. "I try to keep myself fit because I don't want her to start looking elsewhere for attention. Have you ever noticed that after people get married, they usually put on weight? I figure if I can look good for her, she won't cheat on me," he said, revealing the true reason why he obsessively exercised. He wasn't working out for self-improvement, but rather out of fear. Simply put, Patrick believed that if he did not keep his body nearly perfect, Sarah might leave him for another man.

It was becoming obvious that most of Patrick's life revolved around behaviors that were intentionally designed to keep Sarah from leaving him, using money as a tool of control, while foolishly injecting steroids under the misguided belief that his physical appearance alone would keep her interested.

With just a few minutes left on my treadmill's timer, and with it our time at the gym, I wanted Patrick to give further thought to his behavior and to how it might be damaging his marriage. I knew better than to try and get him to see how his childhood experiences were influencing his present. He was simply too upset to revisit this painful part of his life. Instead, I decided to focus on the future, specifically on how he planned to proceed with Sarah and their marriage. I said, "Do you think all of the energy you are spending trying to keep her from leaving might actually be having the opposite effect? Don't you ever get tired of trying to look perfect and spending all of your hard-earned money on steroids?"

He considered the questions briefly before responding, taking a few deep breaths during his deliberation. "I know what you are getting at, and I see your point. Deep inside, I have known this for a long time. Sarah doesn't know this, but I have been living off credit cards and borrowing money just to keep everything going—the house, her, the steroids. There are some days I don't even eat because I am so broke. To tell you the truth, I have even thought about bankruptcy."

He tapped a few buttons to power down his treadmill. "Truthfully, I am exhausted from trying to keep it all together. Sometimes I feel like a hamster on a wheel that does not know how to get off." His treadmill stopped and he looked directly at me. "I think I need to have an honest talk with Sarah about a few things and see how I can fix this."

"How the both of you can fix this," I added, wanting him to understand that both he and Sarah would have to address these problems together.

We finished our workout, grabbed our jackets from the locker room, and headed outside into the star-filled October night, where a cool fall breeze hinted at the approaching winter. As we said our good-byes, he patted me on the back and said, "Thanks for listening, man. You have helped me see some things I hadn't noticed." I squinted my eyes, looking at him with skepticism.

"Okay, okay—you know what I mean. You helped me to start looking at some of my own behaviors. Maybe I can put things right at home. Thanks again." He smiled and quickly added, "See you at the gym soon, okay?"

Without waiting for my reply, he turned around and disappeared into the darkness.

I didn't see Patrick at the gym very much after that evening. The times we did meet, he purposely avoided our intimate discussion, opting instead to make small talk on safe subjects like sports and current events. Months later, however, I heard through the grapevine that he and Sarah had indeed separated. Although I could not be sure, I assumed that she had finally made good on her threat to leave.

So why would Patrick, an intelligent, good-looking, and outwardly friendly guy, need to control his wife through money? Why did he spend so much money on steroids? And why would he allow himself to go into debt? What's more, where did he receive such misguided views about women?

Let's dig a little deeper.

To be sure, Patrick's need to control his wife was unequivocally related to his past. He lived each day in fear that his wife would abandon him, both consciously and subconsciously. When his mother left him at such an early age, Patrick was thrown into the role of caretaker, his father depending on him to attend to the household duties that had once been performed by his mother. When his father became depressed over his wife's betrayal and abandonment, Patrick acted as his emotional crutch, helping him through the grieving process and supporting him until he stabilized.

Who, then, helped Patrick through his time of grief? It is safe to assume probably no one, given that he was so caught up with trying to take care of his father's emotional needs while unintentionally neglecting his own. This may help to explain his misguided views on women. We learn our views regarding gender and assigned roles from our parents, and it is logical to assume that, after his wife left him, Patrick's father influenced and then contaminated Patrick's beliefs about women. To be sure, what Patrick did not learn from his father, he was left to figure out on his own. His rigid views on women represented the anger he had for his mother, displaced onto his wife, and then projected onto the female gender as a whole. But his misguided societal views on women also indicate that he had never fully processed (or accepted) the true reasons why his mother may have left. Although he did not mention it, I suspected that there might have been other factors that contributed to his mother's abrupt departure and caused her to flee into the arms of another man. Perhaps his father employed similar control tactics on his wife, much in the same way Patrick was employing them on Sarah. Was the generational baton passed on from father to son? And while it is true that people can and do walk out on long-term relationships in favor of another person, there are *usually* other issues that can be attributed to the relational collapse. Were there warning signs from Patrick's mother similar to the warning signs that Patrick received from Sarah?

As Patrick entered adulthood, he continued his adopted role of caretaker, coupled with unprocessed feelings of grief and anger. In his marriage with Sarah, he had an overwhelming need to care for her needs, both physically and financially. At some point, his caretaker role became dualistic in nature, and he started to care for his partner *and* to control her. The root of this need to control her began with his terrifying fear of abandonment.

You might think that Patrick treated Sarah as a slave, and in many ways this is true. She was unable to work, go to school, or otherwise partake in activities that made her feel mentally and emotionally fulfilled. She certainly was not made to feel that she was contributing to the marriage with her husband or treated as an equal. But the real slave in this marriage was Patrick, as his life revolved around controlling Sarah through money and his fears of abandonment. He was also enslaved to Sarah physically, spending ridiculous amounts of money on steroids and believing that the investment in his body would somehow make him irresistible to her. In fact, he believed this so much that he was willing to compromise his physical and financial health in order to maintain his body.

Patrick, it seems, was suffering from deeply wounded low self-esteem and thus connected the possibility of keeping love, or trapping love, on his physical appearance. This narcissistic belief is a rather shallow view, to be sure, but it is not uncommon among those of us who confuse love with obsession. Remember, appearances can be deceiving, and sometimes love is just an illusion.

Patrick was "missing the boat" where Sarah was concerned and in many ways had not even tried to catch it. Instead of making her feel valued, he made her feel *devalued.* Instead of making her feel as if she were contributing to their marriage, he had made her feel like a possession. Each time Sarah came to him and begged for money, a little bit of their relationship died. That he looked like "God's gift to the world" meant very little to her, because in time Sarah began to resent him for his ability to monetarily control her. Had Sarah been trusted to work, go to school, and experience the freedom of a loving and trusting relationship, things might have turned out quite differently. This, however, was not to be, as Patrick was unwilling or incapable of taking responsibility for his controlling behaviors.

Money can indeed be used as a tool of exacting control over a partner. If we ever hope to recover from our addiction, we must learn to trust our partners and want them to feel as equals. Before this can happen, we must recognize our controlling behaviors. For those of us actively confusing love with obsession, the following traits and characteristics are commonly present when money is used as a tool of control:

- We adopt the role of financial provider in a relationship, regardless of ability to assume such a role.
- We accumulate debt by paying for a partner's needs while neglecting our own.
- We use money as a way of keeping a partner trapped in the relationship, controlling access to financial resources, including cash and credit cards.
- We spend large amounts of money on a partner, attempting to buy love through self-described acts of kindness. This can include expensive meals, elaborate gifts, clothes, and vacations.
- We willingly assume responsibility for a partner's debts.
- We pay out extraordinary amounts of money on items related to personal appearance because of our low self-esteem. Hoping to keep a partner interested, we will overspend on designer clothes, expensive makeup, stylish haircuts, cosmetic surgery, and drugs (such as steroids) to achieve a certain "look."
- We refuse to allow a partner to pay for basic household needs, such as groceries and household supplies.
- We are not attracted to people who are financially self-

supporting, screening out possible "suitors" who are able to monetarily provide for themselves.

• We will not allow a partner to work for a living, believing that the ability to earn money is a threat to the relationship and can lead to abandonment.

In a perfect world, Patrick's mother would not have abandoned him and would have been there to offer him the proper guidance and support he needed to relate to women in healthier ways. But as we know all too well, *perfect* and *ideal* do not describe our (or most) childhoods. Patrick adopted his role of caretaker the moment his mother walked out the door. As with most people who confuse love with obsession, he continued doing what was familiar to him, marching right into adulthood and performing the role that he knew all too well.

Controlling another person inflicts so many harms— some obvious, some not so obvious. The final sum of that harm can be measured in the tears we cry and losses we endure when that which we have loved or thought we loved is no more.

Once we shed our childhood roles, such as the role of caretaker, we begin to see things as they actually are, rather than through the eyes of a child. The fear of loss and abandonment can indeed be overwhelming, but if we, the relationally dependent, ever wish to embark down a path of healing, we must learn to identify these childhood roles and expose them for what they are—painful echoes from the past where love was cruelly absent through no fault of our own. Once this is accomplished, these echoes begin to grow silent, and in time, we can begin to heal.

4

I HATE YOU,
BUT DO YOU LOVE ME?

For whom have I labored? For whom have I journeyed?
For whom have I suffered? I have gained absolutely
nothing for myself—I have only profited the snake!

—*The Epic of Gilgamesh*

"SHE REALLY DIDN'T MEAN TO HURT ME. She promised she wouldn't do it again, and I think this time she really means it."

"He only hits me when I piss him off. I just have to make sure that I am more careful how I speak to him."

"It's not as bad as it looks—just a few bruises. I'll be okay."

Sound familiar? Those of us who confuse love with obsession commonly use excuses such as these to justify a partner's abusive behaviors. In fact, many of us suffer untold abuses, hiding our secret from the world while living in constant fear. In the end, we find ourselves caught up in associations with people who are emotionally unavailable and extremely abusive. They walk all over us, like a well-worn carpet, as we keep our mouths shut, believing deep inside that if we adjust our behavior, we can somehow control theirs.

Certainly, there is no excuse for emotional or physical abuse, nor is there any justification for it. Nobody deserves to get called names, to be told she is worthless, or to be hit— period. And while we *intellectually* understand this universal truth, many of us feel powerless to make changes when in an abusive situation. Why do those of us who confuse love with obsession find it impossible to walk away from our abusers? Why are we so obsessed with *their needs, their feelings,* and *their welfare,* when clearly they do not truly care about ours? Do we honestly believe that by changing our behavior, we can somehow control theirs?

The bio-psychosocial model of addiction tells us that addictions are holistic in nature, comprised of various genetic, medical, psychological, and sociocultural aspects. Those of us who confuse love with obsession need to closely examine the role of family in the addictive process, acknowledging that childhood experiences are the primary causal factor in our addiction and that these addictive roots can be generations deep. The familial link helps explain why family therapy is considered the "treatment of choice" for most addictive disorders (this is according to Judith Lewis's textbook *Addictions*). Simply put, if our parents dealt with stress by drinking, abusing substances, or hitting one another, we may adopt these same unhealthy behaviors as a way of coping with life's problems. If we are not mirroring our parents' behaviors, it does *not* mean that we have escaped the past unscathed. In fact, some of us have been stricken with a far more sinister form of damage; we assume the role of "peacemaker at all costs." Kate's story is a perfect example of how children who grow up with an abusive parent can find themselves trapped in a similar relationship in adulthood, where continuing the childhood role of peacemaker becomes an unintentional and dangerous tool of control.

I met Kate when she sent me an e-mail regarding an article I had written about addictive relationships. Although I had grown accustomed to receiving dozens of e-mails each day on this subject, her correspondence was particularly trouble-some. In her note she wrote:

> *Dear Mr. Moore:*
> *I am in an abusive relationship with a man. Although I know he loves me, sometimes I get hit for no reason. I am not sure where to turn and would really like some help. I live on the South Side of Chicago and work downtown as a receptionist for a big com-pany. I need to talk to someone about my problem. Is that per-son you?*

We agreed that a safe place for us to meet would be on the Michigan Avenue Bridge, part of Chicago's "Magnificent Mile." Judging by the urgency of her follow-up e-mails, I could tell her situation was desperate. She had already warned me that our time would be limited, writing that she could only meet with me during her lunch hour. We ex-changed physical descriptions of ourselves and picked a day. We met on a warm spring afternoon. The smell of Lake Michigan filled the air as a gentle breeze made its way through the city's concrete canyons. As I rested my elbows on the bridge's rails and watched the sun's reflection bounce off the lake's glistening waters, out of the corner of my eye, I saw a well-dressed woman slowly approaching. I immediately knew it was Kate. Her face was round and slightly tanned, with blond hair tied neatly behind her neck in a ponytail. Her fig-ure was slender and fit, and at twenty-five years old, she could have easily passed as a fashion model. After pausing for a mo-ment to mentally confirm my description, she quickened her steps until she stood next to me, on my right side.

Following mutual introductions, Kate attempted to ease her anxieties by making small talk about the wonderful

Chicago weather and the beauty of the downtown sky-scrapers. Although she tried to appear confident, her facial expressions revealed a deep and hollow pain. I allowed her to avoid discussing the true purpose of our visit until she was emotionally ready to open up.

For a time she remained quiet and reflective, looking out onto Lake Michigan. Several minutes later, against the soft background noise of passing water taxis, she began to speak: "I don't consider myself obsessed with my partner—although after reading your article and being really honest with myself, I'm beginning to wonder."

She swung her head around in my direction. "I've been with this guy named Peter for about three years, and for the most part, we get along just fine. It's just that sometimes—if I catch him in a bad mood, he gets pissed off at me and becomes verbally abusive. When he gets really mad, he hits me. You see, that is the reason I contacted you. Last week I had to drive myself to the emergency room after he threw a full can of beer at my back. I wasn't injured seriously or anything, just a few bruises and a lot of pain but nothing broken," she said matter-of-factly. "I guess he must have had a bad day at work and got angry with me when I didn't have supper on the table when he got home. I know that the best thing I can do is walk away, but I love him so much, you know?" She smiled ruefully and then continued, "I promised myself when I was a kid to never allow a man to treat me this way—the way my father treated my mother."

She paused for a moment and struggled with the painful memories of her childhood. "It's not like Dad hit her every day, but I can remember times when her face was so black and blue that she refused to go outside. I feel guilty saying this, but I am glad my dad died a few years ago—he can't hurt Mom anymore."

She looked away from me momentarily.

"With Peter, I have tried to avoid saying anything that might get him angry with me," she said as she lowered her head. "But I don't think it's working anymore." She then scuffed at the ground with her right foot. "I'm tired of caking on makeup to cover up the bruises," she said, with obvious frustration in her voice.

In order for her to continue opening up, I had to gently prod her for more details, which she reluctantly gave, avoiding eye contact with me: "It doesn't happen every night—but sometimes he flies off the handle and does some pretty rotten things to me. Most of the time, he just yells obscenities at me and calls me names. I hate him sometimes.

"We met a few years ago through a mutual friend, when I was twenty-two," she explained. "He was twenty-five and working for a construction company. He still does that kind of work." She smiled briefly and continued giving me their history. "During the beginning of our relationship, he was so gentle and nice. He would surprise me with flowers and little gifts—you know, the romantic stuff that shows you care." Her eyes lit up as she recalled the memories. "My God, he was so gorgeous—a carbon copy of Brad Pitt. My girlfriends used to joke around with me and tell me he was a 'keeper' and that we should get hitched. You know, he still looks the same way he did when we met." She reached up toward her neck and pulled the collar of her shirt slightly back, revealing a golden, heart-shaped locket that was slightly smaller than the size of a quarter. I leaned forward as she opened it up to examine the tiny photograph inside. The picture was of Peter: short blond hair, penetrating blue eyes, and chiseled cheekbones, complemented by a perfectly square chin. Although the picture was tiny, I could tell that he was a muscular man, capable of overpowering Kate quite easily.

"You are right; he is very handsome," I commented, and she smiled bitterly in agreement, pressing her lips together. She went on to describe the physical demands that Peter's construction work placed on him. According to Kate, it was not uncommon for his workday to start at 4:00 a.m. and end at 4:00 p.m., causing him to come home exhausted and irritable.

"So I try to keep a low profile when he comes home," Kate said. "I usually have dinner ready for him when he walks through the door, and of course the apartment is always spotless. But sometimes, if I have to work late, I am not able to get home before he does; that gets him pissed. I've actually given thought to quitting my job so that I can be home more for him."

Frustrated and now more reflective, she scuffed at the ground again, causing tiny bits of pebble to scatter.

"I am not sure what happened, because he wasn't like this when we first met. It was only after I moved in with him and we settled into the relationship that I began to notice his temperament. Actually, he is nothing like the person I had first met. I know I said this before, but I really should walk away from him."

"Run away is more like it," I wanted to say, but I remained silent.

She continued talking about all of the things that "pissed Peter off," as she put it. She revealed that part of being in a relationship with him meant having to perform certain duties. Kate was expected to do all of the cooking, cleaning, shopping, and laundering. If she did not meet his exact expectations, she was punished. Such punishments might include the silent treatment, verbal abuse, and physical abuse.

Kate gave me every indication that while intellectually she knew her relationship with Peter was unhealthy, emotionally she was incapable of leaving him. As is common with people who confuse love with obsession, there is a place between fear and hope that traps a person in the misguided belief that she can somehow fix her partner. I wanted to know more about why she had chosen to stay with Peter, and so I asked, "Kate, if you know that he is mistreating you in such a horrible way, why are you still with him?"

She took a few moments to think before giving her response: "I don't know, to be honest with you. I think partly because I love him, and partly because I think I can help him change—you know, to become the person he was when we first met. I honestly believe that love conquers all."

"And what if love isn't enough and he keeps abusing you?" I asked.

"That's not going to happen—he will change! He has got to change, or I don't know what I will do." She turned her head toward the lake again, and I could tell that she was holding back tears of pain.

I placed my hand on her shoulder hoping to comfort her, allowing a few moments to pass before continuing.

"Kate, I know this is difficult, but it sounds like you have been trying to change him for some time now and have gotten nowhere. Do you really believe changing him is possible?"

She positioned both hands on the bridge's railing and grabbed tightly. "I've *got* to believe he will change. I don't know what I would do without him." She took a deep breath, paused for a few moments, and said, "Why can't he see how much I love him. I do everything he expects and more. But he still treats me like shit. What am I doing wrong?"

Sensing there was something she was leaving out, I waited a few moments for her to calm down and asked, "Does he drink?"

Before answering my question, she released her tight grip on the railing, quickly turned around, and rested the midpart of her back against the bridge's railing for support. "Sometimes he drinks—but just beer." She proceeded to fumble around in her purse and pulled out a cigarette. After lighting it, she added, "And he drinks a lot of it." She deeply extracted nicotine from the cigarette and exhaled a cloud of bluish smoke. "Usually, I just let him drink until he gets tired and crawls into bed. I *always* make sure there is beer in the house."

"Would you explain why you do that?" I asked.

"About a year ago I went shopping and forgot to pick up his six-pack, and he beat the shit out of me," Kate said.

Increasingly concerned, I asked for more details.

"After work, I went to the store and picked up supper, I think chicken and vegetables." She inhaled more nicotine. "Everything was so beautifully prepared for him that evening. I even had candles on the table." She winced momentarily before continuing, "Well, the one thing that I had forgotten was the beer. Like he does every night, he walked through the door and headed straight for the refrigerator. When he didn't see his 'liquid courage,' he swiped all of the food off the table and lunged at me in an angry rage. Then he grabbed me by my hair and shoved my head into the refrigerator. He kept saying, 'You forgot the beer, bitch!' I told him I was sorry and pleaded with him to let me go—but he was so angry. He kept my head in the refrigerator and then slammed the door repeatedly until I was nearly unconscious. A few hours later, I woke up on the floor, and he was gone—out drinking with his buddies. I went to the bathroom and looked in the mirror and saw that the whole left side of my face was bruised. I had to call in sick to work for five days straight until the swelling went down."

Kate's facial expression turned less serious, and she managed to produce a weak smile. "When he saw what he did to me, he promised that he would never do it again. Well, at least when he gets mad at me, I know he cares, even if he doesn't know how to express it."

Kate revealed her shocking belief that physical abuse was a form of "care," as she put it. Concerned, I gently queried for more details, asking, "But that wasn't the end of it, I take it?"

She threw her cigarette onto the street and continued, "Things were good for a little while, and he actually acted like the Peter I had first met—you know, like the guy who cared about me. But the behavior didn't last very long, because a few weeks after the beer incident, he was back to yelling at me and slapping me around." She made direct eye contact with me and said, "But in a way I deserved some of it, because I did piss him off a few times by saying I would be home to make dinner and then not being able to do it because of work."

Here again, Kate demonstrated just how misguided her beliefs were. In her mind, she honestly believed that Peter's abuse toward her was somehow justified. I wondered if she had set a behavioral boundary with him, and so I asked, "Have you ever told him that if he hits you again, you would walk away?"

"That's why I am here to talk to you. In my mind I know I should leave him. Once, I actually packed a bag and was halfway out the door." She looked away momentarily. "But I chickened out in the end. It's not like I was afraid to leave because he would hurt me." Kate said this, woefully miscalculating the danger Peter presented to her. "If I leave, who will wash his clothes, do his shopping, and take care of him? I know he is a 'big boy,' but he appreciates it when I do things for him." She lifted her head high. "I enjoy taking care of Peter, and when I give him attention, it usually puts him in a good mood. And isn't fighting a normal part of any relationship?" She smiled. "He can really be a terrific guy if he wants to. You know there *is* a good side to him, and that's the part of him I love. That is why I've stayed with him, because deep inside I know I can make him see how he is hurting us. When things are good with Pete, they are *really* good."

"And when they are bad, I try to reason with him even more," Kate could have easily added. At this point in her life, she was incapable of leaving Pete, despite the fact that he presented a very real danger to her life.

We had decided to take a short stroll from the Michigan Avenue Bridge down to the Riverwalk, an area that is near water level and far more private. Once Kate and I reached our destination, we discovered an empty park bench that offered an unobstructed view of the river, with nearby trees offering shelter from the sun. Along the way, I became curious as to why Kate was utterly incapable of leaving her partner. Specifically, I wanted to know how the relationship with her father had influenced her current predicament, given what she had previously reported to me about him. After we sat down, I decided to uncover more clues.

"You mentioned earlier that your father hit your mother. When this happened, how did you cope?" I asked and observed Kate's face as she looked off into the distance. She squinted her eyes, as if searching for something lost.

"Well, there really wasn't much I could do, being so young. Usually, I would grab my younger brother, Sam, and we would run upstairs to my bedroom and shut the door. I remember Mom begging my father not to hit her, but he never listened. But I didn't always run away. Sometimes I would try and protect my mother from Dad's abuse."

"Go on," I encouraged.

"Sometimes when Dad was hitting her, I would grab his arm or jump on his back. I would even call him names, hoping that he would stop hitting Mom and focus his anger on me. My poor mother. You know, all she ever did was clean that house and cook for the bastard. On top of everything else, she was pretty sick most of the time because of her diabetic condition. I remember yelling at Dad and trying to get him to get off of her—begging him to stop hurting her and to leave her alone. And, of course, Mom and I were always on our best behavior to avoid getting him pissed in the first place. When he became violent, we would usually agree with whatever he was mad about and hope that it would quiet him down—you know, as a way of telling him he was right. Sometimes it worked and sometimes it didn't."

It was this last statement that made me suspect that Kate believed that another person's abusive behavior could be avoided, prevented, and even changed. Simply put, she had come to believe that by policing her own behaviors or agreeing with an abuser's point of view, she could somehow make the abuse stop.

"Are all the memories of your father so violent?" I inquired.

"No, Dad could be nice at times. I remember wonderful family trips to the zoo where Mom and Dad would hold hands while Sam and I would accompany them to the different attractions. And then there were the times that Dad would bundle all of us up in the car and take us out for ice cream. Right out of the blue, he would come home from his job at the factory and start tickling us and say, 'Who wants a banana split?' Other times, my father would put his big arms around us and read bedtime stories and give us whisker burns before we went off to sleep. Those are nice memories, and I loved it when Dad showed us love. So I can't honestly say he was a complete monster. I just hated him when he hit Mom."

I asked, "So if he wasn't always a monster, why are you glad that he is dead?"

She raised her right eyebrow, considered the question, and

then answered, "Most of my memories of Dad are negative. Yes, there were good times, but for the most part he treated my mother terribly—and pretty much kept doing it until the day he died. My mother is a good person and did not deserve to be treated that way. So yeah, I was relieved when he died because I knew he could not hurt her anymore. I've pretty much put the son of a bitch out of my mind."

It was getting late, and I realized that she would have to return to work. In the few minutes we had left, I wanted Kate to examine the genesis of her problem by relating the past to her current predicament.

"Kate," I said, gently grabbing her hand, "do you think the relationship you had with your parents, specifically with your father, may somehow be influencing your current situation with Peter?"

She thought about the question carefully and replied, "Yes, I suppose so. I *can* see how part of me is reliving my experiences with Dad through my relationship with Peter. It's weird. I can kind of see myself wanting to change Peter, like I tried to do with Dad—you know, trying to get him to stop the hitting and making things peaceful." She lowered her head slowly. "I never gave it any thought until today."

Her eyes became focused on the ground, almost as if she were in a trancelike state. "My goodness, I guess Dad is still alive today in my relationship with Peter." She reached behind her neck and tugged gently on her ponytail. "This is going to take me a long time to figure out, and I need to get going."

We both arose from the bench, and Kate shook my hand firmly and said, "Thanks for meeting me today. You have given me a great deal to think about. I'm not sure what I am going to do—but I know at some point I am going to do something."

Before she left, I took out a pen from my pocket and jotted

down the number to a domestic abuse hotline on the back of my business card and encouraged her to use it.

"Thanks, maybe I will call," she said. "You've been a great help, and I will e-mail you soon."

Kate left the Riverwalk area and disappeared from my sight. I never heard from her again.

To be sure, Kate had begun to see how her past had influenced her present. However, she still had a long journey ahead of her if she wished to become free of her abusive relationship with Peter.

So why would Kate, a vibrant, intelligent, and attractive young woman, allow herself to be trapped into a physically abusive relationship with a man who posed a real danger to her life? Why couldn't she follow through on her desire to separate from him? The simple answer is she was emotionally incapable of walking away, despite her intellectual awareness. For Kate and many of us who confuse love with obsession, there is a misguided belief that the abuser's behavior can somehow be controlled, changed, even fixed. Let's take a closer look at Kate's childhood and relate her past to her present.

As a child, Kate was forced to witness her mother endure physical (and emotional) abuse at the hands of her father. Feeling helpless, she attempted to stop the abuse by acting as an intermediary, with the hope of protecting her mother. At times, she found this tactic effective, albeit temporary. During those occasional times when her father acted "lovingly," Kate mistakenly believed that this was brought about by her ability to somehow control her father's behavior and bring about peace. Although she did not come right out and say it, I strongly suspected that her father was an alcoholic, given some of his behaviors.

That she was attracted to a man like Peter was no accident, as it is human nature to want closeness with those who are familiar. It is safe to assume that Peter's dependency on beer each night, coupled with his erratic and abusive behaviors, qualified him as an alcoholic too, thereby making Kate a "coalcoholic." Part of being a coalcoholic can mean taking responsibility for the alcoholic's abusive behaviors and then justifying those behaviors through self-blame.

For children, parental security is a powerful and innate need. When that sense of security is threatened by domestic violence, children are often thrust into an adultlike role, where they become a sort of behavioral referee and an emotional punching bag. The role of peacemaker, like most roles that we adopt, is a learned role and one that imprints itself onto the emotional psyche. This is what happened to Kate when her childhood role as peacemaker subconsciously carried itself into adulthood, leading her to believe that abusive men could somehow be changed. In her well-intentioned but misguided attempts to change her man, she even believed that some of the abuse was justified. But what else could she do? The blueprint for how she would relate to men and the role she would adopt in her relationships had been fused into her subconscious long ago during her formative years. Her experience is common among those of us who confuse love with obsession. The roles that we adopted from our dysfunctional childhoods end up revisiting us during adulthood, perpetuating a cruel and never-ending cycle of pain and sorrow.

What Kate did not understand was there is *never* a justification for physical abuse. People who physically abuse their partners are emotional cowards, using fists rather than sound reason to work through problems. Domestic violence is all about power and control, and in Kate's case, Peter was using a twisted form of control in order to keep her "in check." His behavior was inexcusable and reprehensible, and in no way was she to blame for his violent outbursts.

Those of us who confuse love with obsession have a misguided belief that an abuser can somehow be changed into "Mr. Nice Guy." This is not to say that the abuser cannot stop his violent ways; it *is* possible. However, this can only occur when the abuser takes responsibility for the violent behavior. Kate had it all mixed up, believing that somehow physical abuse was to be expected in her relationships with men. She subconsciously believed that if she adjusted and policed her own behavior, she could somehow control and even change Peter's abusive ways. Children who grow up in environments where domestic abuse is prevalent suffer unfair and long-lasting emotional damage. These children are caught up in a storm of fear and confusion, which shatters an environment that is supposed to foster love and stability. When Kate's father hit her mother, he poisoned her soul and negatively impacted her ability to develop healthy ideas about the way men relate to women.

Because, as stated earlier, it is human nature to attach to the familiar, it is only natural to become attracted to that which we understand. Kate was a beautiful young woman who found herself in a situation where her past became her present. The more Peter hurt her, the more she tried to control and change him by adjusting her behavior. In fact, she became so obsessed with changing him that she could not see the dangerous reality of her situation. The truth is that she was powerless to permanently change Peter's behavior, just as she was powerless to change her father's. That she actually believed that some of the abuse directed toward her was warranted demonstrates the severity of the damage inflicted on her as a child. On those occasions when Peter showed affection, Kate attributed this to her ability to control and change him, thereby getting him to behave in a caring way—the way she believed was the "real Peter," as she had described.

Although Kate reported that Peter was not violent in the beginning of their relationship, I suspected that she saw the warning signs early on. Physically abusive men can indeed be "charmers," masking their rage behind acts of kindness and good deeds. In time, however, the mask of charm comes off, revealing a truer and more disfigured face that is filled with anger and rage. Kate's attraction to Peter began when she caught the first glances of his rage, which I surmised first became apparent to her through verbal abuse. The angrier Peter became, the more attracted she became to him. The more Peter tried to control her through violence, the more Kate adjusted her own behavior, hoping to control and change him. Kate's experience represents a vicious cycle for those of us who confuse love with obsession, a cycle that locks the victim into an addictive eddy of control, self-blame, and repetition.

If we are being abused, it is important to understand that physical violence in any relationship is *unacceptable*. When a person slaps, hits, punches, or in any way becomes violent with her partner, it is abuse. When a person punches holes through solid walls, throws around heavy objects, or uses his body size to intimidate his partner, it is abuse. And when a person pathologically violates her partner through acts of violence, the abuse can escalate to the point of serious injury and, in some cases, death. *Violence is never a substitute for love.*

Those of us who actively confuse love with obsession in physically abusive relationships usually exhibit the following characteristics before embarking down a path to recovery:

• We engage in self-negotiation, believing that changes in personal behavior will stop the abuser from inflicting further harm.

- We negotiate with the abuser, believing we can somehow stop the abuse through logic, reason, and understanding.
- We blame ourselves for being physically abused and attempt to "make things better" after a fight.
- We attempt to understand what makes the abuser "tick" and then hope to use that knowledge to avoid further abuse.
- We attribute the "good times" to adjustments in personal behavior, believing that a physically abusive partner can "change" if we show enough love.
- We "walk on eggshells" and live in constant fear of being physically, verbally, or emotionally abused.
- We police our own behavior in order to avoid abuse.
- We minimize or hide the physical abuses that a partner inflicts on us, hiding our reality from the world.
- We minimize, hide, or enable any addictions the abuser may be dealing with.
- We enter into and stay in abusive relationships, thereby perpetuating the childhood role of peacemaker.
- We confuse love with violence, believing that physical abuse is an acceptable form of affection.

Kate's story represents those of countless people who find themselves caught up in physically abusive relationships. All too often, those of us who confuse love with obsession abandon our own dreams, hopes, and desires in a misguided attempt to fix our partner by assuming the role of peacemaker. We live with the daily struggle, hoping that our attempts will somehow make our partner happy and prevent further abuse.

However, once we abandon the role of peacemaker, we begin to objectively look at the relationship for what it is—pain, heartache, and agony. No longer emotionally chained to our abuser, we begin to take stock in ourselves and realize that violence is not a substitute for love and that we are capable of experiencing true security in a mutually giving and supportive relationship. We need to be mindful of the roles that we have adopted in our relationships and then search for any cyclical patterns over the course of time. If the price of love means deep suffering, then love is nothing more than a fantasy, and fear is our reality.

As you continue reading this book, examine the roles of the different people who confuse love with obsession and pay close attention to what speaks to your current situation or pattern. Once you learn to identify your pattern, you will experience the joy of self-awareness and, more important, a step toward healing.

5

LIVING A SECRET LIFE—
CONFUSING LOVE WITH SEX

> After destroying an innumerable multitude of living
> beings, it had propagated itself without respite from place
> to place, and so calamitously, had spread into the West.
>
> —Giovanni Boccaccio, *The Decameron*

I WALKED INTO THE HOSPITAL ROOM that evening with
his file, expecting to see him lying in an inclined bed and
propped up by a set of pillows. Instead, he was sitting still in
a chair, gazing out the window of his private room while
watching the purple autumn sky grow dim as the sun disappeared behind the city's skyline. Tears were running down
his face as he twisted a piece of paper in both hands.

Tom, a thirty-four-year-old midlevel business executive
had been admitted to the hospital a week earlier after his doctor became concerned over a dangerously high temperature,
coupled with extreme fatigue and chronic diarrhea. Sitting in
his chair, he looked totally unattached to reality.

To let him know I was in the room, I placed the file I was
carrying on the window's ledge.

"So you are my case manager? I am sorry you have to see
me like this," he began, taking a few tissues from a box on a
nearby table and blotting his eyes. In a gesture of support, I
pulled up a chair and sat down next to him, resting my hand
on his shoulder.

"Yes, I am," I said, gently squeezing his shoulder and looking into his eyes.

Tom took a deep breath and began to tremble, trying to work up the courage to speak. Tears continued pouring from his eyes, and his lips began to quiver. Several moments passed before he was finally able to speak.

"I have AIDS," he gasped, turning his head away from me. "They did some blood tests a few days ago, and I got the results yesterday."

As he continued to weep, I gently took the piece of paper that he had been nervously twisting in his hands. It was a lab report, confirming his AIDS diagnosis. Scribbled on the side of the report, a hospital staff person had written

HIV POSITIVE
AIDS DIAGNOSIS—OPPORTUNISTIC INFECTION
MYCOBACTERIUM AVIUM COMPLEX (MAC)

"I still cannot believe this—I have AIDS! I am freaking out and losing control, and I don't know what to do." However, it was his next comments that helped me gain more insight into his current predicament.

"I have no idea who I got this from. I have slept with so many guys that it could have been from anyone." His voice cracked as he tried to choke back the tears. "I should have known better, but I guess this was bound to happen. Can you help me? Can anybody help me?"

I had been assigned to Tom's case because his physician had referred him to the social services agency I worked for to receive case management services. Part of opening a new case with a client involves conducting a psychological/social assessment, where background information is recorded, including but not limited to childhood history, medical history,

history of relationships, access to financial and medical re-sources, educational background, and, if present, addictions. After spending time with Tom and listening to the responses to the various intake questions, I began to suspect that he was struggling with two distinct but related dependencies: an addiction to relationships and an addiction to sex. From what I could ascertain, he would have anonymous sex with multiple men to bolster his self-esteem and counteract his deep depression, which worsened during times of stress in his relationships.

The term *sex addict* is widely misunderstood and often not discussed because of social taboos, coupled with igno-rance on the part of many mental health workers. To in any way think that Tom's sexual orientation is behind his sexual addiction or his HIV diagnosis is to be gravely misinformed and, worse, perpetuates ignorance. Sex addicts can be straight or gay, male or female, young or old, and of any race and eth-nic background.

According to Patrick Carnes, Ph.D., author of *Out of the Shadows: Understanding Sexual Addiction,* a sexual addiction can be compared to other addictions, such as alcoholism or a dependency on other drugs. Much like a heroin addict needs a "hit" to feel normal, a sex addict needs a sexual encounter to "feel" whole. For some people who confuse love with ob-session, a coaddiction with sex *may* be present. To be sure, many relationally addicted people do not suffer from this de-pendency, but for those who do, the recovery process must address both addictions.

Tom continued expressing his grief and shock, "My life has been hard enough. Why is this happening to me? Haven't I suffered enough? I paid my dues when I was a kid."

I already knew from the intake questions that when he was ten years old, his parents were killed in a car accident, and he became a ward of the state. It wasn't until he was fifteen that he was placed in a permanent foster home. I suspected that this traumatic childhood experience had left Tom emotionally scarred, strongly affecting the way he approached both sex and relationships later in life. I remained with him for several hours that evening, allowing him to share his grief and to express genuine feelings of anger.

Several weeks after he was released from the hospital, I stopped by his home to discover his emotional progress and to further determine his needs. After we discussed the various benefits available to him, he began to talk about his predicament.

"The doctors have asked me to start making a list of my recent sexual partners. I guess they want me to call them all and tell them to get tested," said Tom, who was sitting across from me at his dining room table. "The list will be pretty long. I've been 'active' since I was nineteen years old."

"Would it help you to talk about that time of your life?" I asked gently, hoping to discover the details of his past while building trust.

Tom cleared his throat and then began to speak: "I earned nearly perfect grades in high school and somehow was awarded a scholarship to college. Not bad for a kid who grew up a ward of the state. It was so great because I was able to live on my own because the scholarship paid for everything. I couldn't wait to get away from my foster parents because they just kept me in their house for the state's money. In fact, there were six of us living there, and it was always a game of competition to gain their attention.

"I had figured out I was gay long before college, having a few sexual experiences here and there, but I had never really dated anyone." He cleared his throat again. "So about three months into my freshman year, I met this guy named Craig in a finance class, and I was immediately attracted to him. After he figured out I was interested in him, he asked me out a few times, and we started dating seriously. I couldn't keep my hands off of him. We would have sex almost every day; he was so handsome." Tom managed to produce a faint smile while recalling the memory. "It was like Cupid shot me with his arrow because I fell seriously in love with this guy. Deep inside, however, I couldn't help but feel that he was just in it for the sex. After a while, he lost interest in me sexually and started pushing me away. I was afraid of losing him, so I tried to make the relationship more interesting."

"How so?" I asked.

"I used to get him drunk or high and then invite other guys over for three-ways. I figured that he liked all of the sexual attention and that at least I could keep him around, if even just physically. Pretty soon, though, my little tricks didn't work, and he broke up with me anyway. Losing him was devastating, and I felt totally rejected."

It was this revelation that made me further suspect that he had an addiction to relationships and a coaddiction to sex. That he used sex as a means of manipulating his partner into staying with him represented a strong fear of abandonment, coupled with feelings of low self-esteem. It made perfect sense to me, however, given that he had lost both of his parents at such a young age. The collapse of his first significant relationship and the events that surrounded it subconsciously reinforced his fears.

"It must have been hard for you," I commented, wondering how this pattern would continue.

"It *was* hard—until I met this boy named Steve. I guess you could call him the transition guy. I met him through a mutual friend and found him to be very attractive. We were kind of hot and heavy for a few months, and I really liked him, but I was still feeling pretty depressed over Craig. But he was a warm body to sleep next to, and it made me feel less lonely," said Tom, the color of his face turning a faint hue of red.

"I was still having sex with different guys, although Steve didn't know it." He then looked directly at me and smiled ruefully. "I used to make him promise not to screw around with other guys on me. That was sort of selfish on my part, seeing that I was playing around behind his back all the time. Don't get me wrong, it's not that I did not care for Steve; it's just that I was still dealing with the breakup with Craig. The end of that relationship came when Steve found out I was having sex with his best friend. He dumped me right away, and I was all alone—again."

Tom's sexual behavior during this time period was to be expected, given his fear of abandonment caused by the death of his parents. Suffering such a trauma as a child stripped away his chance of experiencing the love and support he needed to build the foundation for healthy relationships in the future. Void of this parental love, Tom had come to believe in his subconscious and conscious mind that anonymous sex with strangers in adulthood was a way of creating personal closeness, without fear of desertion. When he did find himself in a relationship, it was usually based on a physical attraction and was in many ways superficial. As Tom grew older and his unhealthy pattern of relating to men continued, sex and love would combine to form a powerful addictive vortex, creating a storm that would eventually destroy everything in its path.

"I have not told anyone about this yet, not even my foster parents," Tom said. "You don't just call someone up on the phone and say, 'Hi, how are you and by the way I have AIDS.' I might not ever tell them, because all it will do is make them ask questions that I do not have the answers to—you know, like 'Who did you get it from?'

"I have thought of telling some of my ex-partners, but I am not sure if I am ready to do that because I am afraid of how they might respond." He paused for a few moments to consider his dilemma and then continued, "On the other hand, I do feel a responsibility to tell them so they can get tested."

Indeed, Tom did have a responsibility to tell his partners of his HIV status. Revealing the truth, however, would mean having to also reveal a very secret part of his life. As with most people who confuse love with obsession, this can prove to be difficult.

He continued speaking and giving more clues: "I've had a few days to think about this, and I guess this is not really a big surprise. Basically, I have been living a lie for the past ten years, kind of like having a double life."

"What do you mean?" I asked.

"Well, after college I avoided relationships like the plague. Oh sure, I dated a few guys here and there, but nothing serious. If I was horny, I could always go to an adult bookstore or pop in a porn. It wasn't until my late twenties that I started dating again. That's when I met David, a gorgeous hunk who caught my attention at a bar. After about six months of dating, he told me over drinks one night that he loved me—those magic words again. I had not heard those words spoken for years, and I couldn't believe such a hot guy was into me.

"He asked me to move in with him, and I immediately said yes. At first, everything seemed so perfect, but that did not last for long. I still had a hard time believing that this guy was into me and wondered if he was just interested in me because I made good money." His face contorted while he struggled with the difficult memories. "I used to grill him big-time about where he was during the day, fearing that some other guy had gotten his slimy paws on him. I really got into that guy."

Tom stopped speaking for a few moments to retrieve the coffeepot from the kitchen, returning shortly with two freshly poured cups.

"I was definitely addicted to him to be honest," said Tom, revealing his true sentiments. "We did not have all that much in common—except for the sex. He was an actor and part-time model. Trying to have an intelligent conversation with him was pointless, because all he understood was his small corner of the world. We had completely separate interests. I was into current events, stocks, and business. He was into working out, music, and fashion. I had to dumb myself down at times so that we would have something to talk about.

"But David made me feel secure and needed. At that time in my life, I thought being in a relationship would help me stay grounded. I even managed to stay monogamous for a few months. But as we settled into the relationship, infidelity reared its ugly head.

"It first happened when I was on a business trip to Seattle. I was bored, so I pulled out my laptop and started cruising the Internet. Before I knew it, I was on some Web site that featured local escorts. I hired two of them to come over, and we had a three-way. I figured it wouldn't hurt anybody, so why not? But when I got back from my trip, I kept cheating.

"I would rent a hotel room across from my office down-town and hire escorts to meet me for sex during the lunch hour. If I could get a half day off work, I would trot on down to the bathhouse and spend a good four to five hours there. It was like I was in a trance when I was there, doing all sorts of sexual stuff—mostly unsafe. It just felt so good to connect with people like that—you know what I mean? If I couldn't get time off, I would cruise the bathrooms at the department stores during lunch, sometimes finding other guys who were willing to play. It was kind of like a daily ritual: I would dress up in my business suit for the office and look like the usual corporate 'execudriod,' but during the lunch hour I would sneak off to different places looking for sex. When co-workers would ask me out to lunch, I would make up excuses and tell them something silly, like 'I am going to meet a friend.'"

I continued listening to him, allowing him the chance to relate his sexual addiction to his relationship with David. "I always felt guilty after I 'got off' with someone, and that's probably why I used to accuse David of cheating on me. I think it's called *projection,* if I recall my psychology courses in college. We would get into fierce fights on the weekends, or when we were together for long periods of time, because I would accuse him of cheating while I was at work during the week. He would deny it vehemently, sometimes getting so pissed with my interrogations that he would storm out of the apartment. When he would come back, I would try to smooth things over by having sex with him and making him promise to remain faithful." He laughed softly. "Sex after a fight is always the best, if you know what I mean."

"Did you have safe sex with David?" I asked, trying to sound nonjudgmental.

"Are you serious? No! I never had safe sex with him. If I started wearing condoms, he would have become suspicious. And, of course, I never made him wear one. Trying to keep my 'other' life secret was hard. It was like walking a tight-rope, twenty-four hours a day, seven days a week. With David, I was 'hooked on the look' and didn't want to lose him be-cause he was so hot."

The relationship that Tom shared with David was dys-functional, as were all of his previous relationships with men. Without realizing it, he had revealed that his addictive attachment to David was purely physical and in many ways served to bolster his self-image through a misguided form of validation. While Tom's attempts to hide his "secret" sex life from David were self-serving, they were also very manipulative. The fact that he expected David to remain monogamous and berated him about alleged sexual encounters typified Tom's need to control the relationship. As with most people who confuse love with obsession, a moment occurs when the addict's behavior can no longer be concealed, and the truth becomes apparent.

"Things really started to get out of control toward the end of the relationship," Tom continued. "I was out looking for sex almost daily, and if I wasn't looking for it, I was thinking about it. The more I tried to hide it from David, the more suspicious I became of his own behavior, I think, because of guilt. After telling so many lies, I was having a hard time keeping my stories straight. And of course, the fights were getting worse. There was so much tension in the relationship that it was almost unbearable. Things went from bad to worse.

"I started having sex with this other guy from work, if you can believe that! We would meet in the bathroom at lunch and sneak into an empty stall. I used to really like meeting him there because it was an easy way to . . ." Tom stopped talking for a moment and then continued: "Then one day he and I were doing the nasty, and we heard a tap on the stall door." Tom paused here to take a sip of coffee and then shook his head. "It turned out to be the building's security. There were two guards with walkie-talkies outside waiting, and the third one was posted in front of the restroom, barring others from entering. I guess someone had heard us and snitched. Me and the other guy were so scared. By this time, everyone I worked with had gathered outside the men's room to see what all the commotion was about. I just about died when one of the guard's walkie-talkies blurted out a message at full volume that said, 'Bring the two perverts who were having sex in the bathroom down to security room four.' Of course that caused all of my busybody co-workers to start whispering. All I could do was keep my head down as they took us away.

"I begged security not to call the police. I didn't want to have someone come bail me out of jail. They agreed to not call the cops, but I did end up paying the price for what I had done."

"How is that?" I asked.

"To begin with, security and building management wanted me to sign some piece of paper that basically asked me to never again set foot on the property. I told them I worked for a company located in their building, but they were not interested." Tom laughed derisively before continuing. "It didn't matter anyway, because I had no intention of ever going back to my office again. Everyone knew what I had done. I signed their document and walked out onto the street. Gone was my job of fifty thousand dollars a year—just like that.

"There was no way I could tell David why I lost my job, so I told him that I was 'let go' because of cutbacks. That excuse worked for a few days, until a human resources 'bitch' left a message on our voice mail at home. She called to ask me how I wanted my personal belongings to be handled—the stuff on my desk that I was unable to retrieve. In her 'lovely' message, she reminded me that I could not enter the building to pick up these things because of the 'incident.' Of course, David heard the message before I did, and that's when the 'shit hit the fan.' He became suspicious and talked to a co-worker of mine and found out the whole truth. I had no choice at this point but to confess. I told him why I got fired and begged him not to leave, promising him that it was just a 'onetime thing' and to never ever do it again. I knew that I was lying, but I did not want to lose him. Things were never quite the same after that, and I think it is fair to say that all the trust he had in me was blown."

Tom became quiet for a few moments while he recalled the difficult memories. He then continued his story: "So a few weeks after getting busted, I started looking for work. At that time, I was on my best behavior, going straight to the interviews and then coming right home. But I was so stressed out about my relationship with David, plus looking for a job, that I needed a release.

"One day when David was supposed to be at work, I asked this guy I had met on the Internet to come over. I was bored, you know? After he stopped by, we went to the bedroom and started kissing. Before I knew it, we were having sex. I remember looking into the mirror that was hanging on the wall while we were playing. The reflection looking back at me was of the one person I did not want to see—David! He had come home from a play rehearsal early, and I had not heard him enter the apartment.

"Well, that was the last straw for David. He packed up his things that day and moved in with one of his friends, leaving me in the apartment all alone. He made sure to call me a 'whore' before he left, which hurt a lot. Everything happened at once—the job and then David. Talk about a double whammy."

"How were you able to cope with all of that stress?" I asked.

"I really wasn't able to cope. Even though losing the job was hard, it wasn't half as hard as losing David. My life turned into this horrible, slow-motion nightmare. For the first two days after he walked out on me, I couldn't even get out of the bed. I tried calling him a couple of times on his cell phone, but he never picked up. I think I lost ten pounds in the first two or three weeks after he dumped me.

"After a while, I got sick of leaving voice-mail messages and hoping for a call back. So I got myself together and went out to the bars at night to get drunk so I could forget about my problems. Usually, I would end up going home with someone or spending the night having sex with guys in an adult bookstore.

"I was an emotional wreck and was in no condition to be job hunting. Most of my days were spent down at the bathhouse, where I would rent a room and screw around with God knows how many people. I just didn't want to be in that apartment, surrounded by all of those memories. I was so depressed that I would let people do whatever they wanted to me, which including screwing me without a condom. I didn't care."

Here we see a classic example of how a person who confuses love with obsession deals with loss when suffering from a sexual coaddiction. Long ago, Tom had learned that having sex with strangers was a way of coping with stress, loss, and depression. When his addictive relationship with David was forced to an end, his coaddiction with sex escalated. The causal reasons behind his behavior were twofold. First, Tom lost his primary means of self-validation when his relationship with David ended. Because Tom believed that David was "extremely good looking," as he put it, he was bolstering his own self-worth through their relationship. So when the relationship ended, so did his sense of esteem, which he sought to bolster through these sexual encounters. Second, Tom became extremely depressed when the relationship ended, which also made him act out sexually, as a way of coping with the pain. Specifically, having anonymous sex with strangers was his way of feeling needed once again. Although misguided, it also made him feel loved.

Tom went on, revealing the depths of his addiction to David: "So I went through this phase where I started having sex with guys that David used to be involved with. I knew all of his old boyfriends and would call them up on the phone to come over for 'drinks.' If I pushed it, we would end up having sex. I did this not so much for revenge, but as a way of being close to David. I kind of figured that by sleeping with his exes, I would still be attached to him in some way. Sick, huh?" He opened his mouth to say something more, but then stopped himself.

"Is there something more?" I asked.

"Yes, but I am embarrassed." His next words were spoken in whispers. "When I would go to the baths, I would have sex with people and imagine they were David. Sometimes while I was looking through the shadows, my mind would play tricks on me. It was like I was hallucinating or something." Tom paused for a moment to gather his thoughts and then continued, "I would stand and watch this total stranger having sex with someone else and believe one of them was my David. Part of my mind was telling me, 'This is not real,' but I swear there were times when I honestly believed David was right there in front of me. When this would happen, I would usually try to get the guy that looked like David to screw me. Isn't that weird?"

On the surface, Tom's hallucinations may appear to be symptomatic of a larger psychological issue, such as psychosis. His experience, however, was quite normal for a person who confuses love with obsession. In fact, his hallucinogenic experience represents a common form of relational withdrawal.

Deprived of the powerful emotional association with his former partner, Tom began to subconsciously project David's physical characteristics onto others. Because he suffered from a coaddiction with sex, his withdrawal symptoms became sexualized. His desire to engage in sex with David 'look-alikes' served to fill the psychological and physical void that the relationship once satisfied. His need to have sex without a condom represented his extreme state of denial, causing him to want to experience closeness with someone without regard for his safety.

There are other psychological and physical withdrawal symptoms that those of us who are relationally dependent may suffer from during times of loss. These withdraw symptoms may include the following:

- An inability to sleep or erratic sleeping patterns
- Shaking or tremors
- Severe restlessness
- The chills (caused by decreased circulation)
- Increased anxieties
- An extreme loss of appetite
- An overwhelming feeling of "electric fleas" on the skin (itching)
- Chronic diarrhea
- General disorientation to time or place
- An inability to concentrate

A defining characteristic of addictive behaviors is that they involve the pursuit of short-term gratification at the expense of long-term harm. To be sure, Tom was harming himself both emotionally and physically while at the bathhouse, yet he remained ambivalent to the self-inflicted damage. Each anonymous sexual experience fed his addictive cycle, increasing the need for more of the "drug," in this case, sex, while he struggled to maintain emotional stability.

For those of us who are relationally dependent *and* sexually addicted, a direct threat to our health can unintentionally become a turning point. Tom's health threat occurred in the form of an HIV/AIDS diagnosis. This represented a crucial turning point that forced him to embark down the road of self-awareness, which ultimately led him to seek help.

Tom concluded his story with the following: "I think this AIDS diagnosis was a wake-up call. I am going to get myself some help by going to counseling and attending a support group for people like me. I have been looking on the computer and found a group that deals with sex and love addictions. I guess that is what you could say I am—an addict. For the time being, I am going to avoid any new relationships until I get a grip on my problems. I know it is going to be hard, but I am going to try to stop having sex with people. I have to do this. I can't live this way anymore."

Months after my visit with Tom at his apartment, Tom began to improve physically with the help of antiviral medications prescribed by his doctor that helped to prevent new incidences of HIV-related illness (opportunistic infections). He was even able to return to work, thanks to advances in the treatment of HIV.

Tom's story represents the extreme outcome of a person who is relationally addicted while suffering from a coaddiction to sex. Ideally, Tom would have received the love and support he needed as a child, which would have enabled him to build the proper foundation for meaningful, healthy relationships in adulthood. This was not the case, however, as his world was destroyed at the age of ten when his parents were taken from him. Without this proper foundation, he unintentionally assigned misguided emotional and psychological meaning to sex and relationships. In short, Tom was confusing love with sex, which ultimately caused both to become an obsession.

So how do we know if we or someone we love is living with a sexual addiction? Before examining some common traits and characteristics, we must first rule out the common misconceptions. An individual is *not necessarily* a sex addict if he exhibits one or more of the following characteristics:

- Has a healthy sexual appetite in a committed and loving relationship
- Has a nocturnal emission during sleep (wet dreams)
- Occasionally masturbates (different from habitual)
- Occasionally uses erotic images for stimulation (different from dependence)
- Uses sex toys or experiments with different sexual positions
- Wants to have sex with his partner often

In order for a person to qualify as having an addiction, she must meet the criteria outlined in the *Diagnostic and Statistical Manual of Mental Disorders (DSM-IV-TR, or DSM).* This manual, published by the American Psychiatric Association, provides key diagnostic criteria for substance dependence, which we can adapt for our purposes to sexual addiction. Here are three of the criteria:*

- A great deal of time is spent in order to obtain the substance (e.g., looking for sex online for hours at a time, driving long distances in order to find sex, or leafing through sexual imagery during much of the day).
- Important social, occupational, or recreational activities are given up or reduced because of substance use (e.g., missing or

---

* These are only three of the seven diagnostic criteria used to diagnose a substance dependence problem as defined by the *DSM.* Currently, only three criteria are required to occur within the same twelve-month period in order to be diagnosed with substance dependence.

being late for work in pursuit of sex or skipping family events because of a need to obtain sex or sexual imagery).
• A persistent desire is present to cut down on the substance or control the substance (e.g., unsuccessfully trying to cut down or stop the compulsive pursuit of sex or sexual imagery).

With these criteria in mind, let's look at the common traits and characteristics of the relationally dependent person who is also addicted to sex. (A sex addiction *can* exist independent of other addictions, but for the purposes of this book, we will focus on the relationally dependent sex addict.) Please note that these characteristics are not a complete list. A few of these traits are taken from the nonprofit group called Sex and Love Addicts Anonymous.

COMMON TRAITS AND CHARACTERISTICS OF A RELATIONALLY ADDICTIVE PERSON WHO SUFFERS FROM A SEXUAL COADDICTION

1. Becomes sexually involved with and/or emotionally attached to someone without knowing the person*
2. Gets involved in one relationship after another, sometimes being involved in more than one emotional and/or sexual relationship at a time†
3. Equates love with sex and seeks sexual experiences as a way of feeling needed
4. Uses sex and emotional involvement to control others‡
5. Passes all intimate relationships with others through a "sex

---

* Adapted from *Addiction and Recovery* pamphlet, Sex and Love Anonymous, 1992.
† Ibid.
‡ Ibid.

test," meaning that closeness with another person is based on sex or the possibility of sex

6. Acts upon sexual fantasies with a partner's friends or former lovers, hoping to live vicariously through the experience

7. Searches compulsively for and engages in anonymous sex with others

8. Spends compulsively or excessive amounts of money on sex or sex-related materials, causing or contributing to debt

9. Attempts to involve a partner in group sex (three-ways), hoping that this will somehow "save" the relationship and keep a partner interested

10. Demands monogamy from a partner yet is unable to offer the same

11. Makes career choices based on the availability of sex

12. Masturbates habitually and may develop a dependence on pornography in order to be stimulated

13. Receives self-validation through the relationship, which is primarily built upon sex

14. Uses sex as a way of dealing with stress, depression, and rejection, sometimes having sex with strangers as a way of bolstering self-esteem

Upon closer examination of Tom's behavior, we can see that he exhibited nearly all of the characteristics of a relationally dependent person who suffers from a coaddiction to sex. That he gained his self-worth through intimate relationships and anonymous sexual experiences indicates a dual-addictive paradigm, which is unique to relationally addicted persons. Some of us who confuse love with obsession find ourselves living a double life, attempting to keep our partner from abandoning us while searching for love with strangers.

In Tom's case, his addiction to the relationship with David was so overwhelming that, when it was forced to end, his coaddiction to sex went into overdrive, and he went on to have multiple anonymous sexual experiences with others, with little or no regard for his emotional and physical safety.

What's important here is to understand that, like alcoholism and other drug addictions, relationship and sex addictions are *diseases*. Diseases do not go away on their own but require the help and support of others to overcome. It is also important to point out that these addictions are treatable. While there is no cure currently available, there is recovery. Many resources and tools are available to help the addict live with the problem. Much of what is presented in this book is aimed at recognizing addictive behaviors with the hope of planting the seedlings of change.

In Tom's case, he made good on his promise to seek help, primarily with the help of a therapist who specializes in relationship and sex addictions. He also joined a support group that provided a nonjudgmental and supportive environment for sharing. As he learned more about his addictions, he discovered that his views toward relationships and sex were "backward," as he later described them to me. He was only able to reach this place of self-awareness when he began to recognize and accept his unhealthy behaviors and to commit himself to ongoing support and treatment.

It would be wrong for me to say that Tom is truly free from his addictions. It would be more appropriate to say that Tom has remained relationally and sexually sober because he has committed himself to a path to recovery, with the help and support of others. That is the reality for people who suffer from any addiction—be it gambling, a chemical dependency, or sex and love addictions. They *never* go away; they are lived with.

Being in love should not mean being in pain, and living fully should not mean having to lead a double life. Our childhood experiences, the role of family, and societal influences play a large role in the way we approach relationships later in life. Let's continue examining others who confuse love with obsession, paying special attention to these important influences.

6

THE TOOLS
OF CONTROL

I know not—but if truth, I will confess it.

—Euripides, *Ion*

WHAT ARE SOME OTHER, LESS OBVIOUS WAYS that people who confuse love with obsession might use to keep their partners shackled to the relationship? How, for example, does the relationally addicted man use food to break down his wife's self-esteem, with the goal of keeping her chained to him? How can an obsessed wife use manipulation to keep her man homebound? How does a husband use psychological violence against his wife to keep her emotionally dependent on him? What role can alcohol and other drugs play in the controlling process? And how can an addicted parent use her child as a pawn in a dysfunctional marriage?

Before exploring the answers to these questions, we must first recognize that those of us who confuse love with obsession suffer from a disease, which in many ways is similar to alcoholism or a chemical addiction. The name of this disease is *relational dependency,* and the definition that follows is a variation of Marty Mann's definition of alcoholism as presented in her book *Primer on Alcoholism.*

Relational dependency is a disease process that manifests itself primarily through an uncontrollable obsession with another person, which causes the dependent person, also known as the addict, to become engrossed and preoccupied with the object of his obsession. If the relationship continues, the disease grows more powerful, eventually overwhelming the addict and causing him to plummet into a vortex of obsession. This intense and disturbing preoccupation with another person disassociates the addict from reality and impairs his judgment. The only two eventual outlets for this disease are psychosis or recovery.

This disease concept of relational dependency is an important concept to understand if recovery from the addiction is ever to be achieved. Why? Because understanding that we have a disease allows us to see our obsessive behaviors as an illness—a condition we do not choose to have. If we can accept this reality, we can then distance ourselves enough from our controlling behaviors and move on to identify and examine our actions through the act of self-reflection, with the goal of making the subconscious conscious. This is not an easy task, as most of us have spent a lifetime in denial about our behaviors, blaming the world for our misfortunes, while accepting little or no responsibility for our misdeeds. But understanding the nature of the illness is paramount and lights the metaphoric torch of hope on the path toward recovery.

Perhaps the easiest way to embark down the road of self-reflection is to examine the controlling behaviors of others who struggle with an overwhelming need to control a partner. Some of the stories that follow are from men and women who are actively working on their recovery through support groups such as Sex and Love Addicts Anonymous (SLAA), Co-Dependents Anonymous (CoDA), and Incest Survivors Anonymous (ISA). Other stories come from people who, although not in recovery, wanted to share their tools of control with the hope of helping others. It is important to remember that it is not uncommon for some of us who confuse love with obsession to be struggling with a coaddiction and that any attempts at recovery must address all dependencies. While reading about these addicts, please note the common theme behind the behaviors: a fear of abandonment.

Some of the control tactics, or tools of control, may be difficult to read about because they speak to your own experience. When this happens, put the book aside and return to it later when you are emotionally able to continue. It is important to read each story carefully to recognize any particular patterns in your life with either past or present relationships.

Because there are so many different ways a person can manipulate a partner, it is simply not possible to list every single tool of control in this book. What appears here are some of the less obvious but nonetheless insidious ways that some of us have used manipulation in an effort to keep a mate attached to the relationship. For easier behavioral identification, the primary tool of control has been isolated and identified. This in no way implies that relationally dependent people do not use multiple tools of control, because in fact many of us do. However, for our purposes, we will examine these individually. Keep in mind, while reading the following stories, that relational dependency is a progressive disease that makes the addict do *anything*, no matter how hurtful or bizarre, to keep another attached to the relationship.

Richard

PRIMARY TOOL OF CONTROL: Food

Age: thirty-seven. Relationally sober for two years. Mother was a drug addict who died when he was fifteen of an unintentional opiate overdose. Going through a divorce.

When I first met Karla, she was a total knockout. She exercised almost every day and really watched what she ate. But because of my addiction to her, I purposely sabotaged her appearance, which ended up destroying our three-year marriage.

I can still hear passersby making remarks to her like, "Hi, sexy," or "Damn, you are fine." The whistling and catcalls from construction workers drove me up a wall. In fact, my buddies used to tell me to keep a close eye on Karla because she was so "hot." Well, all of the attention she received made me feel pretty insecure inside and extremely afraid that she would meet someone new. I didn't want to lose her because she brought meaning to my life and a sense of belonging.

So to bring a halt to all of the attention she was receiving, I secretly devised a plan to fatten her up. But before I could do this, I had to first stop her from exercising. To do this, I started berating her for wanting to go to the gym, accused her of cheating, and in any way I could, made her feel guilty for trying to maintain and improve her appearance. I remember saying things to her like, "Who are you trying to impress?" and "Who are you cheating with at the gym?" At first she put up a fight and tried to reason with me, but my guilt trips eventually won and she stopped heading to the gym after work. That's when I started with the food.

The once healthy meals she used to cook were replaced by my disgusting antics in the kitchen. Everything I prepared for her was purposely loaded with carbohydrates, starches, sugars, and greasy fats. I actually read somewhere that carbohydrates were addictive, so I made sure I always prepared heavy meals, like meatloaf. I would even fatten up normally healthy foods, like fish, by dipping them in lard or butter before cooking it in oil. And of course, I always served dessert, which I made sure included her favorite flavor—chocolate. So that I wouldn't put on the extra pounds, I would eat smaller portions of what I cooked and secretly exercise during my lunch hour at work. Karla didn't know this because I told her that I had canceled my gym membership to make time for her.

At first, Karla bitched about what I was feeding her and complained that it was causing her to gain weight, but I countered this by accusing her of insulting my cooking. It seemed like guilt always worked with her. In time, all of the stuff I was doing to get her fat worked because she stopped griping and ballooned from her normal 139 pounds up to 200 in no time. And of course, with each new pound she gained along the way, her self-esteem decreased. I remember being so happy about what I was doing—knowing that she wouldn't be hit on as much by other guys.

At some point, however, she became deeply depressed. She would ask me how I thought she looked, complaining that none of her clothes fit anymore. I would lie to Karla and tell her that I liked her "big" and that she would always be gorgeous to me, no matter how she looked. I had bouts of guilt for what I was doing but rationalized my behavior by thinking to myself that married people don't need to worry about how they look and that she was happier being fat. But when Karla reached 210, she became extremely depressed and went to a therapist for help.

After a few sessions, she and her counselor figured out what was really happening, given that I hadn't gained a pound since the day we met. When she confronted me about her suspicions, I, of course, denied everything and told her that she was out of her mind. Then one night I came home and she was gone, with a note left on the refrigerator telling me that we were getting a divorce. She wrote it on the back of a current bank statement that showed that my gym membership had been recently paid. My fear of Karla leaving me came true—but not because she was cheating on me. The divorce isn't final yet, but it will only be a matter of time. I know now that my addiction to her made me act in such a disgusting way, and all I can do is ask for her forgiveness.

Why Richard Used Food as a Tool of Control

Richard's use of food as a tool of control against his wife is not uncommon among people who confuse love with obsession. As a child, he lost his mother because of her addiction to drugs. Her early death from an accidental opiate overdose imprinted within his subconscious a deeply held fear of abandonment, which would later become the ultimate driving force behind the manipulation of his wife's appearance. Although Richard's behavior was underhanded and deceitful, it is important to dissect the behavior from the actual person— in other words, "Hate the addiction and not the addict." That his wife received positive attention for her appearance represented a terrifying threat to his marriage, which he viewed as a threat to himself. This caused him to become anxious and insecure, harkening back to similar feelings he experienced as a child when his mother passed away. Not wanting to experience another painful loss in his life, he used food as a tool of control to change his wife's appearance, hoping to keep her undesirable to others.

After his wife divorced him, he went into an immediate crisis. It was then that he began to examine his manipulative behaviors and seek help. The word *crisis* comes to us from the Greek word *krisis,* which means decisive moment. For virtually all of us who confuse love with obsession, crisis is the point in time where change is most likely to occur, because this is when we begin to take a mental inventory of our controlling behaviors. This inventory, in turn, causes us to weigh what we have lost against what we have gained through our manipulative actions. This insight forces us to realize that we must change our behaviors or be left on the self-destructive path of heartache and pain. Richard was no different during his time of crisis. He sought out therapy and joined a support group for people like himself who manipulated their partners to keep the person attached to the relationship. With the support of others, he learned that he suffered from a disease that caused him to engage in behaviors that in many ways were beyond his ability to control. He also learned to forgive himself for what he did to his wife and to eventually ask for her forgiveness. By sharing his tool of control with others in his support group, Richard gained special insight into his addiction and took the first step down a path to recovery.

Gretchen

PRIMARY TOOL OF CONTROL: Manipulation

Age: twenty-nine. Daughter of an alcoholic mother. In therapy for six months. Divorced with two boys who are in the custody of their father.

I was married to Nick for about five years, and we had two sons. The first few years of our marriage were pretty good, and he treated me like a queen. The boys adored him, and he spent a lot of time with them—you know, showing affection and making them laugh. We were all so happy together. But our happiness was short-lived because four years into our marriage, things changed.

He was employed as a computer technician and was very good at what he did, so when a new job came open where he worked, Nick was tapped to fill the position. I can still remember him coming home that night and announcing with pride that he had been promoted. I was happy for him, until I heard that the new job required occasional out-of-town travel. The first five-day trip he took away from home was difficult for me, and I guess you could say that I freaked out. I can remember feeling so anxious, waking up in the middle of the night only to find myself lying alone in an empty bed. Sometimes, I would lie there and become paranoid, wondering whom he was sleeping with while he was away. I guess my fears got the worst of me because when he got back from his trip, I accused him of using the business trips for cheating purposes. He tried to tell me that I was wrong and to relax, but I wouldn't listen to him.

As time went on, my anxieties grew worse and I literally could not sleep at night because he was not there with me. It was pure hell because when he was at home, I would suddenly wake up in the middle of the night to make sure he was next to me. I mean, he never gave me any real indications he was cheating, but at that time I just figured he was doing it. In any event, I couldn't handle the anxiety and panic attacks anymore, so I decided to do something about it. I started spreading rumors about him to his business associates, telling them that he was sleeping around with some of the customers. I even broke into his laptop and started deleting customer e-mails. I realize now how bad this was, but I wanted to get him fired so he could find another job that allowed him to be home more. It was also around that time that I started saying some pretty nasty things about Nick to the boys— telling them that Daddy was the "bogeyman." I figured that if the kids started pushing him away, he would feel guilty and want to quit his job to be home with them. Although they were too young to talk, they eventually began to cry whenever Nick came around to pick them up. I felt so guilty. I remember wanting to undo the damage, but it was too late.

One afternoon, Nick came home and told me that he was fired for "unprofessional" behavior. The company didn't tell him the specifics surrounding his termination, but I knew why. Three weeks after he got let go, I confessed to what I had done one evening over a heated argument. I just blurted out that I was spreading rumors about him. I also confessed to what I was telling the boys about him. Needless to say, Nick went ballistic. He grabbed the boys and took off in the car for his parents' house. I tried to apologize to him as he drove away, begging him to come back—but like I said, it was too late. A month later, I got the divorce papers with his request for custody. I didn't have a job and was not in a financial position to care for the children. I lost everything because of my behavior—my husband and my children.

My therapist and I figured out that I acted that way toward Nick because of crap that went on during my childhood. Mom was drunk all the time and passed out on the couch. Dad was never around because he purposely worked long hours to avoid being at home with her. I always felt so alone as a kid and hated that feeling. It hurts too much to talk about this anymore.

Why Gretchen Used Manipulation as a Tool of Control

Gretchen's actions toward her husband and children can be blamed on her coalcoholic addiction. During Gretchen's childhood, her mother was emotionally, and many times physically, unavailable to her because of the struggle with alcoholism. As a result of her mother's addiction, Gretchen became a coalcoholic, with two classic characteristics of this family disease: a strong fear of abandonment and an overwhelming need to control others. And what of Gretchen's father? He, too, can be considered a coalcoholic who denied that his wife had an addiction. Instead of being there for Gretchen, he avoided the situation by spending a lot of time away from home, which translated into further abandonment for Gretchen.

As Gretchen physically grew into adulthood, she was emotionally trapped in the past. Her marriage with Nick was doomed from the beginning because she viewed the marriage as an extension of herself. In other words, she tied her identity and self-worth to her marriage rather than to herself. Subconsciously, Nick had become her emotional savior, making her feel whole and needed whenever they were together. His time away from home, however, brought to the surface repressed, painful memories of abandonment from her difficult childhood. Without Gretchen's conscious awareness, these powerful feelings became the driving force behind her destructive, manipulative behaviors. That she purposefully sabotaged her husband's career and used her children as weapons against him represent just how afraid she was of being alone. Now in therapy, Gretchen is beginning to learn why she behaved in the manner that she did, primarily by examining her past.

Dan

PRIMARY TOOL OF CONTROL: Psychological violence

Age: forty-two. One year in recovery with Co-Dependents Anonymous (CoDA). Married for five years with no children. Father was physically abusive. Mother died when he was two.

I met Judy innocently enough one evening when I spotted her in an aisle of our local grocery store. I am not sure where I got the courage, but I walked right up to her and introduced myself, which eventually led to a date. In no time, we discovered that we had a lot in common and started seeing one another exclusively. Both of us had just come out of really bad marriages and were feeling pretty lonely, so the time we spent together chased away the blues. I think the thing that attracted me the most to Judy was her sense of self-confidence and outgoing demeanor. In fact, my therapist told me that that is why I glommed on to her so quickly.

Within three months of meeting, we eloped and Judy moved into my apartment. At the time, it seemed like the right thing to do because of the way we had hit it off, but in hindsight it was a huge mistake. After our short-lived honeymoon, all of the happy feelings we once shared quickly disappeared. Like I said, she was pretty outgoing and so naturally had a lot of friends coming into the marriage. That didn't sit well with me because I wanted her to be with me and nobody else. I realize that sounds selfish, but at the time, that is how I felt. Because of this, I started giving her the silent treatment whenever she talked on the phone to others, be it co-workers, family, or friends. Other times, just to screw with her mind, I would say something really shitty to her like, "I can see why that ex-husband of yours divorced you; you never spent any time with him." Deep inside, I guess I was feeling neglected, and I am still trying to understand why.

In time, my behavior made Judy fearful of saying or doing anything that might get me pissed. My therapist tells me that I had made her frightened and even emotionally dependent on me because she was not allowed to talk to anyone else. It makes sense, because she started asking for my approval for everything—even to go grocery shopping. After about a year of marriage, she threatened to walk out on me, saying that she couldn't handle living this way anymore. Can you blame her? So rather than go through another divorce and lose her, I promised to talk to someone—which at the time I called a "head shrink." The truth is, I knew I had a problem but did not know what it was.

After a few sessions in counseling, my therapist made me see that I used emotional abuse as a tool of control because of my feelings of inadequacy, which apparently stemmed from the way my dad treated me as a kid. You see, Mom died when I was two, and he was the person who raised me. Dad always called me worthless and used the back of his hand against my face to keep me in line. And of course, his drinking habit played a large part in the way he mistreated me—and the way I mistreated myself. Judy and I are still married, and she is now attending therapy with me because my counselor says that she should be part of the treatment process.

Why Dan Used Psychological Violence as a Tool of Control

Dan, like so many of us who had an abusive parent, found himself unable to stop the cycle of violence as he grew into adulthood. It is a common misconception to believe that children reared by physically abusive parents grow up to inflict physical abuse on others. The truth is that children who grow up abused are more likely to be abusers, but not always physical abusers. Why? Violence does not necessarily perpetuate itself in the same form in which it was inflicted upon us.

The genesis for using any kind of abuse against a partner can be traced to the deepest regions of our "hidden self," where past childhood transgressions, often resulting from parental abuse or neglect, become amplified in adulthood through the need to control. Fueled by a fear of abandonment and strong feelings of insecurity, these potent feelings can express themselves in the form of psychological violence, which is commonly directed toward persons we love. In fact, this is exactly what happened to Dan in his marriage to Judy.

When Dan was a child, his abusive father stripped him of the opportunity to develop healthy views about himself. Instead of receiving paternal encouragement and love, he was offered anger and rage. Instead of receiving praise for his achievements, he was offered ridicule and criticism. Is it any wonder that he was attracted to the very characteristics that he did not possess? It is human nature to associate ourselves with that which we desire. In Dan's case, he was attracted to Judy's self-confidence and free spirit, which, in fact, was really her own sense of self-love. Unable to experience this kind of love, Dan locked on to Judy under the misguided belief that she could fill his deep and gnawing void. Afraid to lose his emotional "life preserver," he used psychological violence as a tool of control to restrict and limit Judy's platonic relationships. His deeply held fear of abandonment, coupled with feelings of relational insecurity, can, indeed, be traced to the deepest regions of his hidden self.

The hidden self is that part of our personality that we conceal from the world (and often from ourselves). In many ways, this hidden self is like a small child, trapped in the past and unable to move into the future. Unable to relate in a healthy way to the world that surrounds it, the hidden self lashes out in anger in an effort to exert control. As Dan continues down his path to recovery, he will no doubt learn more about his hidden self and, what's more, his need to use psychological violence as a tool of control.

Mark

PRIMARY TOOL OF CONTROL: Alcohol and other drugs

Age: thirty-four. In a two-year relationship. Both parents were alcoholics.

It had been almost one year since I broke up with my former partner, and I was feeling kind of low. A friend of mine, who was sick of hearing me complain about being lonely, convinced me to accompany him to a local video bar. I guess he thought it would lift my spirits. But there's nothing more miserable than being depressed and having to listen to a group of happy, gay men singing show tunes on a Saturday night. So there I was, nursing a vodka tonic and watching *Oklahoma!* on the video screen while everyone else sang along.

Just when I had all that I could handle and was about to leave, someone bumped into me, knocking my drink to the floor. At first I was angry—until I turned around and saw that the guy who bumped me was a total hunk. Michael (as I learned his name was) apologized and quickly offered to re-place my drink. Immediately, I was taken in by his sense of humor and beautiful smile. We started talking and learning about one another's interests—the normal stuff people do when they first meet. We were the same age, but he could have easily passed for twenty-something. Because both of us worked in retail, we had lots in common. In fact, we had so much in common that before I knew it, we had gabbed for al-most two hours straight and closed the bar. We exchanged telephone numbers and ended the night with a passionate kiss.

I remember wanting to hear Michael's voice again; it was so sexy. But after two days of waiting for him to call and him not doing so, I decided to break my "hard-to-get rule" and dialed his number. He seemed glad that I had called, and it sounded as if he wanted to get together. We made a date for later that evening, deciding to take in a movie and "tie a few on" afterward. When we hooked up, he acted completely dif-ferent than he did the night we first met. I couldn't put my finger on it, but he didn't seem very happy. I didn't want to pry, so we watched the movie in silence and then headed out to the bar. Magically, after he put down a few beers, the happy Michael I had first met returned. He was smiling, making jokes, and basically acting wild—which was very appealing to me. When we left the bar, we went to my place and made passionate love. In fact, it was the most passionate sex I had ever had. The next morning when I woke up to make coffee, I saw him lying in my bed looking so perfect. It was then I knew I wanted to have a relationship with him.

After about three months of dating, Michael and I decided to live together and rented a one-bedroom apartment. It was then that our problems began. He wanted to go out every night and get "toasted," but I wasn't into that. When I said I wanted to stay in, he started sulking around the house and became really depressed. Other times, he would become angry with me and push me away. I had already figured out that Michael was an alcoholic, but it really didn't bother me. I was just so happy to have someone in my life again. Things got worse, however, and we started arguing and fighting every night. I thought he was actually going to walk out on me one Friday evening after we got into a punching match.

So to keep the relationship alive, I decided to give in and use his drinking to my advantage. Not every night, but most nights we were out at the bars getting smashed. At first it was great because he was so full of energy and easy to talk to. And of course, when we returned home at night, the sex was great. But after a while, it got kind of old. He started drinking around the apartment and passing out on the couch. I was getting pretty sick of it, because it seemed all he did was sleep and work and drink. I figured that if I gave him something else to get high on, other than alcohol, he might start acting a little more upbeat and passionate. I just wanted my Michael back—that funny guy who made me happy.

So I asked a buddy of mine to hook me up with some cocaine one day as a favor. One evening after supper, I asked Michael if he wanted to try a few lines. Sure enough, he snorted three lines in succession and was "wired." We ended up having sex and then heading out for a night of drinks and dancing. I liked Michael when he was high because he was easygoing and less serious. Pretty soon we started experimenting with all sorts of drugs. In fact, we did the entire "alphabet," going from cocaine to Ecstasy, all the way up to ketamine and GHB.

Then one night, Michael started having some pretty bad chest pains, and I called an ambulance. When we got to the emergency room, he was in very bad shape. His breathing was slow and labored, and his face was ashen. The doctor said that his heart was racing and that they had to give him some medications to slow it down. I remember being extremely upset and frightened but too high on coke to comprehend the seriousness of the situation. Luckily, they were able to save him that night. One of the nurses told me that had I waited just a few minutes more in getting him there, he might have died.

Today, both of us have cut way back on our partying with drugs, but we still drink pretty heavily. Someone suggested that we go to a therapist or join AA [Alcoholics Anonymous], but we are not ready to do that. It never worked for my parents, so why bother?

Why Mark Used Alcohol and Other Drugs as a Tool of Control

Mark's story depicts an extreme form of relational dependency, where using chemical substances to control another becomes part of the addictive process. His relationship with Michael is a form of infatuation, meaning that he experienced high levels of passion around his partner but low levels of intimacy. This is often the case with those of us who confuse love with obsession; we immediately cling to another without really getting to know the person. Think of it as a twisted version of "love at first sight." Mark's self-described passionate sex with Michael should *not* be confused with lovemaking. During altered states of consciousness, where alcohol or other drugs become part of the mix, it is common to experience powerful feelings of euphoria. What Mark was really experiencing when under the influence was "illusionary intimacy," where he projected his own fantasy of the experience onto his immediate reality.

That Mark became instantaneously attracted to Michael, despite Michael's addiction to alcohol, gives us important clues to his past. As explained in earlier chapters, it is human nature to relate to and be attracted to those who appear familiar. Although he did not reveal the specifics of his childhood, it is logical to assume that his parents were alcoholics, based on his statement, "It [AA] never worked for my parents." Is it *really* that surprising that he glommed onto Michael so quickly? His dependence on Michael to make him feel happy speaks to the silent pain of so many relationship addicts, where the need for self-validation is destructively achieved through painful associations. In short, looking to others, rather than within, became his source of validation.

So why would Mark use Michael's addiction to alcohol to further his own emotional needs? Simply put, he was addicted to the newness of the relationship and the high of being with someone who he thought made him happy. Whenever Mark sensed a threat to that perceived happiness, he manipulated the situation to maintain relational homeostasis. His enabling behaviors toward Michael were extremely self-serving, because his sole desire was to replace self-love through a relationship with another person. He controlled Michael by using his partner's addiction to alcohol to get what he needed to feel whole—affection. When booze didn't work, he escalated his manipulative behaviors to include cocaine and other party drugs—whatever he could use to control Michael. And to be sure, the suggestion that Mark also attend AA was right on target, as he, too, is chemically dependent.

For some of us who confuse love with obsession, alcohol and other drugs can indeed be used as a tool of control. They are perhaps the most dangerous tool because they can damage the mind, body, *and* soul. If we truly wish to be free from relational dependency, we must take into account this particular method of control and seek treatment for any chemical addictions that may also be present.

Beth

PRIMARY TOOL OF CONTROL: A child

Age: twenty-five. Molested by her father. Married with one child. Attends Incest Survivors Anonymous (ISA) every week. In therapy for one year.

I met Stan when I was eighteen years old at one of my younger brother's baseball games. Like me, he was there watching his kid brother strike out. We had caught one another's eye across the field and somehow ended up bumping into each other at the concession stand. After making some small talk, we decided to take in the game together on a quiet area of the bleachers. We both had recently graduated from high school and were of the same mind-set about college: "not interested." We just wanted to find jobs that paid enough for us to escape our parents' homes and think about our education later.

After the game ended, we made a date for a few days later to check out a carnival in a nearby town. I remember thinking about Stan all day after we left the ballpark because he was so handsome. So when the day arrived for us to meet, I was extremely nervous. I really liked him and wanted him to feel the same. I was so nervous that I ended up spilling a soda all over my jeans. He was a perfect gentleman, offering to get napkins and drive me back to my parents' home for a change of clothes. After our time at the carnival, I pretty much knew Stan was the guy for me.

We were married one year later and ended up moving into a trailer. With him working at an all-night convenience store and me staying at home with our seven-month-old baby girl, it was all that we could afford. We named our baby Robin because she was an "unexpected" bird that flew into our life. Living in the trailer was not fun, but the joy our daughter brought into our lives made it bearable. And I tried to make our home as nice as I could. Nothing fancy, of course, but we had plenty of food and decent furniture. Our plan was to save up enough money to buy a starter home, so by the time Robin was five, she would have a decent place to live.

But things turned sour when I began to suspect that Stan was cheating. One night after he got off work, he called me and said he would be late because he had to go to his parents' house and visit his mom who was sick with cancer. I was always a little distrustful of him though, because I used to see him "checking out" other women when we were in public together. Well, he ended up not coming home that night and, in fact, didn't even call. So when he came strolling through the door at seven-thirty in the morning, I was a total wreck and pissed. He told me that he had ended up spending the night at his mother's house because he was too tired to drive back home. I didn't believe him, and we got into a huge fight. Robin started crying, and I remember picking her up and telling her, "Daddy doesn't love you anymore," and "You are going to get a new poppa. Momma is going to find someone who won't hurt you." I said these things at the time because I knew how it would affect Stan. He loves Robin more than anything else in the world, and the thought of losing her made him nervous. But this wasn't the first time she got caught in the cross fire. Anytime we would get into an argument, I would threaten him by saying that I would take Robin away and he would never see the two of us again. It was all so ridiculous, looking back. Things came to a head though, which made me put things into perspective.

When Robin was three years old, Stan and I got into a fierce fight over his "wandering eye." At the supermarket he was checking out some girl, and I could almost swear he smiled at her. Anyway, when we returned home from shopping, I picked up Robin and told Stan that if he ever looked at another woman again, he could kiss his daughter good-bye. He started yelling at me and even called me a bitch. That's when I scooped up Robin and ran outside to the car. Stan came running after me, and in my hurry to get away, I tripped over a rock and dropped Robin onto the concrete. She started screaming and crying, and when I picked her up, I noticed that her left arm was swollen and scraped. Stan and I rushed her to the emergency room and waited for what seemed like hours to find out what was wrong. The doctor told us that she had broken her arm in three places and we were lucky something more serious hadn't happened. It was then that I knew I needed help. I had been using Robin as a pawn against Stan, and she ended up getting seriously hurt because of my insecurities.

I have only been in therapy for about a year now, and my therapist hooked me up with a support group for people who survived what I did. You see, when I was a little girl, my daddy used to come into my room at night and crawl into the bed with me. I really don't want to get into everything that happened, but I think you can put the pieces together. I am just beginning to realize that because I didn't have any control as a kid, I started controlling the things I could when I got older.

My husband is a good man, and I realize that my suspicions were pretty silly. Just because a man looks at another woman, it doesn't mean that they are sleeping together. I am still trying to figure all of this out, but for now, I will just take things one day at a time.

Why Beth Used Her Child as a Tool of Control

Beth's insight into her addiction was extremely accurate. When she was a child, her father stole from her the most sacred possession a child can have—innocence. As a result, fear, uncertainty, and anger were the pervasive feelings during much of Beth's early years. Who wouldn't be insecure in a relationship after enduring what she did? What's more, who wouldn't look to control something after emerging from a childhood void of control? Simply put, Beth is not to blame.

Whenever a child is molested by someone, be it by a parent or other caregiver, the child usually presents the following characteristics in adulthood: feelings of low self-esteem, strong feelings of repressed anger and mistrust, extreme anxiety, and a strong need to control others. Beth exhibited all of these in her relationship with Stan. She was insecure in her relationship with Stan primarily because she was insecure with herself. Using Robin as a tool of control, especially when delivering ultimatums, amplified that part of her hidden self.

In therapy and through the support of others in her group, Beth is starting to process her painful past. Tragically, the damage inflicted on Beth penetrated parts of her psyche that will take years of therapy and support to uncover. Her controlling relational orientation can be traced directly back to horrific memories of molestation when she was a child, and the need to control another in adulthood occurs through no fault of her own. In a perfect world, Beth's father would not have violated her and instead would have provided her with the foundational support she needed in order to grow into an adult with a positive self-view. But this was not to be, and she became the victim of her father's unspeakable abuse, which would later haunt her as she grew into adulthood.

Part of treating relational dependency must take into account those harms that were inflicted on us as children, including harms such as Beth's. This means validating our experiences and not minimizing the pain. Once this happens, we can then move on to something more challenging—forgiving those who have harmed us. This is easier said than done. Once accomplished, however, the true light of healing will begin to illuminate a magnificent, liberating path to recovery.

Controlling another person involves a great deal of energy. If we wish to be truly honest about our addiction, we must recognize our specific tools of control and accept responsibility for having employed them. Self-examination, as with any task that has us look inward, can be a difficult and painful process. It doesn't happen overnight and may take years to accomplish fully. Much of what we experienced as children has been repressed so deeply within our hidden selves that no amount of therapy is going to successfully draw out all of our suffering. We do, however, have a responsibility to ourselves to seek out that which is buried inside. Why? Because our strong need to control another person eventually destroys the very life that we so desperately wish to preserve—our own. Our relationships with our partners, our children, and ourselves are dependent on our ability to become truly self-aware.

The person we are today is the direct result of the person we were yesterday, and the day before yesterday, and so on and so on. We must look inward for clues to the person we are and validate the harms that were inflicted on us in the past. Remember, however, that our past does not define us. With each new day, we have the opportunity to create change, and with that change, self-renewal.

In the following chapter, we will examine the specific attachment styles of the person who confuses love with obsession and the experiences and perceptions of the person being controlled.

THE OBSESSIVE
LOVE WHEEL

> What heart had I left me, during all this,
> or what ought I to have had, except to hate life
> and wish to be with my dead subjects.
>
> —Thomas Bulfinch, *The Age of Fable*

WITH MORE THAN SIX BILLION PEOPLE roaming this planet, how did we manage to find *them,* the objects of our affection? What random act of the universe caused us to cross paths with these people and to ultimately become obsessed with them? More important, what are *their* experiences, feelings, and perceptions as our relationship with them continues and eventually deteriorates?

As mentioned in the previous chapter, those of us who confuse love with obsession suffer from a disease that causes us to behave in ways that are often beyond our control. Before examining the experiences of others involved with a relationally dependent person, it is important to understand how an unhealthy attachment to another evolves over the course of time. I have termed this process Obsessive Relational Progression (ORP). There are four basic but distinct phases of ORP, each characterized by specific behaviors. To illustrate these phases, I have created the Obsessive Love Wheel (OLW). I chose the term *wheel* because this cycle is a state of

constant turning, round and round, as the relationship continues. Sometimes the wheel turns quickly, other times slowly,
but the wheel is always turning and is always painful.

Does this wheel look familiar?

ORP PHASE ONE: THE ATTRACTION PHASE

This initial phase of the relationship is characterized by an
immediate and instantaneous attraction (or attachment) to
another person. Often, all those of us who confuse love with
obsession need to be thrust into this phase is the *slightest* bit
of attention from another. It is at this point that we become
suddenly "hooked" on the object of our obsession.

For those of us who are relationally dependent, the following traits and characteristics are usually present during
the attraction phase (also known as the honeymoon period):

- An overwhelming attraction to another person, usually occurring within moments of first meeting.
- Unrealistic fantasies about the object of our obsession, which can include wild thoughts of eternal togetherness and the assignment of saviorlike qualities to this person.
- An immediate urge to rush into the relationship regardless of compatibility. Warning signs, or red flags, about the other person are often overlooked, including abusive behaviors or an obvious addiction (such as chemical dependency, a gambling addiction, or an eating disorder).
- The beginnings of controlling behaviors.

ORP PHASE TWO: THE ANXIETY PHASE

This phase is considered a relational turning point and usually occurs after a commitment has been made between the parties. Such commitments can include monogamy, engagement, or marriage. Sometimes, however, those of us who confuse love with obsession will enter into this phase without the presence of a commitment. This happens when we create an illusion of intimacy, regardless of the other person's feelings. It is during this phase that the following behaviors usually occur:

- Unfounded thoughts of infidelity and emotional betrayal based on anecdotal evidence, such as a partner coming home late from work.
- An overwhelming fear of abandonment. Baseless thoughts of a partner suddenly walking out on the relationship begin to creep into daily activities.
- Strong feelings of mistrust begin to emerge, which cause us to become depressed.

- High levels of anxiety, characterized by a short temper and angry outbursts.
- Generalized depression, coupled with lethargy.
- Very careful behavior around an unhealthy partner as an attempt to avoid abuse, because we cannot walk away.
- The continuation and escalation of obsessive, controlling thoughts and behaviors.

ORP PHASE THREE: THE OBSESSION PHASE

This particular phase is typified by a rapid escalation of the disease process. It is at this critical point when extreme, obsessive activities begin to become apparent, ultimately overwhelming our life. Phase three is characterized by a total loss of control of personal behaviors, leading to extreme anxiety. Nothing matters at this point other than making a connection with the object of our obsession. In this stage, the following traits, characteristics, and behaviors are usually present:

- "Tunnel vision," meaning that we cannot stop thinking about the object of our obsession.
- Neurotic, compulsive behaviors, including rapid, successive telephone calls to the object of our obsession's place of employment or residence.
- "Drive-bys" of a partner's place of employment or residence, with the goal of assuring ourselves that the person is "where he is supposed to be."
- Physical stalking behaviors, including secretly following the object of our obsession throughout the course of a day to discover the person's daily activities.
- Initiating contacts under false pretenses with friends, family members, acquaintances, or co-workers for the purpose of finding out past and present activities.

- Surreptitiously monitoring a partner's financial affairs, usually through electronic means. Monitoring activities can include unauthorized access to the person's e-mail or online banking records.
- The possible use of violence against the object of our obsession (also includes psychological violence).

ORP PHASE FOUR: THE DESTRUCTION PHASE

This is the final phase of the Obsessive Relational Progression. It is during this phase that the ultimate destruction of the relationship takes place, resulting from phase-three behaviors, which have caused the partner to flee. This phase is characterized by the rapid escalation of existing coaddictions (including addictions to sex, alcohol, and drugs) to compensate for the loss of the relationship. This is the most dangerous of the four phases because we generally experience intense anger and rage, coupled with strong feelings of self-hatred. It is at this point that our body begins to physiologically internalize immense stress, wreaking havoc on the gastrointestinal system, central nervous system, and immune system. Some relationally dependent persons have reported making suicide attempts during phase four because of overwhelming depression. Usually, the following traits, behaviors, and characteristics are common during phase four:

- Overwhelming depression and lethargy.
- Relational withdrawal symptoms, including body tremors, chills, loss of appetite, an inability to sleep, diarrhea, and constipation.
- Hallucinations. We see or hear our object of obsession. Memories of the person oftentimes serve as the hallucinogenic.
- Vivid dreams regarding the object of our affection.

• Extreme feelings of self-hatred, coupled with self-blame.
• Suicidal thoughts or suicide attempts.

How many times have we cycled through these various phases in our relationships? And how might a partner feel when interacting with us? Perhaps the best way to examine what it is like to be on the receiving end of one of these phases is through the other side of the looking glass.

What follows are interviews with the former partners of people who confuse love with obsession. While reading their stories, try to identify which stage of ORP the addict was (or is) in while paying special attention to the perceptions and experiences of the person being controlled.

Randy

SITUATION: Out of a relationship for one month

Age: thirty-one. Carpenter by trade. Never married.

I met Jackie over the Internet on a community dating board. She was twenty-nine, and her picture looked pretty nice. From the biography she wrote, we looked like a match. Because we both liked bowling, we decided to play a few games at a local alley and see where things went. We had a good time on that first date, and I told her that she was very attractive. But after going out a few more times, I noticed she was starting to say some things that were kind of strange. For instance, on our third date she started asking me about what kind of woman I would like to marry and if I wanted to have kids. I was like *whoa*—hang on there a minute! I liked her, though, and wanted to keep seeing her. But when she started saying things like, "I am so glad that you are a part of my life" and "We were meant to be together," I kind of freaked. Mind you, we had only known one another for a month at this point.

Things got really strange when we returned home from a bar one night a little drunk and had our first sexual experience. I remember her saying, "I love you" and "I've been waiting for you my whole life." When I didn't tell her the same thing back, she got angry with me. All of it seemed a bit weird to me. How could she have loved me after only knowing me for a few weeks?

Well, about two weeks after our first sexual experience, she started questioning me about my whereabouts—you know, like we were an exclusive couple. Now how freaked is that? Don't get me wrong, I liked her and everything, but she was moving *way* too fast for me. So one night, she got really pissy with me when I told her that she was weirding me out with her behavior. I told her that I wanted a little time to myself and that we should take a step back and cool it. She called me a "player" and some other names, comparing me to her old boyfriend. After she pulled that, plus the controlling stuff, I was through with her. She called me a few times after that and tried to pull a guilt trip, but I held my ground. The girl was just too needy for me.

Randy and Jackie's Relationship

If you guessed Randy was involved with a person who was in phase one of ORP, you were correct. Like most young men, he was looking to meet someone new and see how the relationship progressed. In fact, he is what you might call a "relational connoisseur," a person who casually dates different people and gets a feel of the relationship *before* making a commitment. His relational pattern, more cautious and slow, is actually quite healthy. But for people such as Jackie, and others who confuse love with obsession, healthy relational patterns do not exist. She went to the extreme, charging full force into the relationship and immediately falling in love with her fantasy of Randy without getting to know him first. She set herself up for great pain by prematurely pouring out her heart and soul and expecting him to do the same. When he did not mirror back the feelings she expressed, she became insecure and hurt. Soon afterward, she began to exert control.

Randy's negative reaction to Jackie's instant, emotional attachment style was understandable. The old adage that "Water and oil don't mix" really is true when discussing attachment styles. His initial attraction to her was physical, while hers was emotional. He wanted to *experience sex* with her, while she wanted him to *make love* to her. Do you see the difference? Those of us who confuse love with obsession must be mindful of our attachment style and how our actions and reactions toward another are perceived by the object of our affection and carefully monitor our actions and reactions to another where matters of the heart are concerned. If the attachment is instantaneous, paradise may actually be nothing more than an illusion.

Tina

SITUATION: Broke up with boyfriend a year ago

Age: twenty-eight. Airport ticket-counter agent.

I used to think Ted was a great guy, but he turned out to be a major creep. The day we met, I was working the boarding gate for the one o'clock flight to Boston. I remember him waiting in a never-ending line for his boarding pass, looking sharp in a custom-made business suit. I knew he was sweet on me because he kept smiling at me the whole time he was waiting. When he finally made his way up to the counter, he was nervous because the flight was getting ready to depart. After I checked him in, he told me that he was heading out East for a business trip but would be back in a week. It was then that he discreetly passed me his business card while giving me a compliment about my appearance. As he ran toward the Jetway, he turned around and held his hand to his ear, pretending to be using a telephone and mouthed "call me." I guess I was pretty naive because I phoned him shortly after he returned. Was that ever a mistake.

When we first started dating, he was a complete gentleman. He paid for everything whenever we went out and refused to allow me the chance to chip in. His job as a stockbroker offered him a great lifestyle, and I guess he felt he had some kind of an obligation to take care of everything. But after we started dating exclusively, I started to feel as if I were owned. About six months into the relationship, over dinner one night, he told me that he believed I was cheating on him and that I owed him the truth because of how good he was treating me. I asked him where the hell he got that from, and he said that he just had his suspicions. I found it odd that he would say such a thing, especially since he knew that I was working twelve- and fourteen-hour days because of cutbacks at the airline. Then there was that freaky note he left me. He must have slipped it in my purse one night while I was sleeping, because I never saw him put it there. While eating lunch with my co-workers, I reached into my handbag for a cigarette and felt a piece of paper. When I pulled it out, I knew right away it was a note from Ted. It read, "Don't cheat on me, baby. You know how much I love you—please don't ruin what we have." That was kind of scary. And then he started making me account for my time, asking me where I was going and calling me a liar no matter how I answered. I had to be careful with every word that came out of my mouth at this point in the relationship because I was afraid it might set him off on one of his cheating tangents. It got to the point that whenever we were together, all we talked about was how I was spending my time and who I was spending it with.

I pulled the plug on the relationship when he snapped at me in front of my co-workers at an employee holiday party. I was talking to a male friend of mine and gave him a hug to wish him a Merry Christmas. In front of everyone, Ted walked right up to me and called me a "cheating little bitch." I thought he was going to take a swing at the guy, but my friend took off before anything happened. It was positively the worst day of my life. I remember running outside in tears and several of my girlfriends gathering around to offer support. I was so embarrassed. When Ted came outside to see what I was doing, I told him to take a hike and that we were finished. I am glad I did because my life is so much better without him.

Tina and Ted's Relationship

Here we see the classic example of someone on the receiving end of phase two of ORP. Is it any wonder Tina wanted to dump Ted, despite his good looks and wealth? He made her feel like a possession, projecting his own fears and insecurities onto the relationship and controlling Tina by making her account for her time. In fact, his insecurity with the relationship caused him to become increasingly frustrated, which made him become angry whenever Tina could not prove her whereabouts to his satisfaction. The fact of the matter is, she could have provided a sworn affidavit from a Supreme Court justice, and he still would not have believed her. Why is this true? Because Ted's relational style of attachment was based on fear and mistrust. As the relationship continued, these feelings grew stronger, ultimately causing the relationship to implode. Ted was incapable of trusting Tina because he was too caught up in the *idea* of infidelity rather than the actual act. This then leads to the questions: Whom did Ted really mistrust? And what part of his past caused him to relate to women in this way?

Tina's reaction to Ted was more than understandable. Nobody likes to watch every move and word she says to avoid an angry outburst from a partner. Having to report her daily whereabouts to Ted must have been extremely frustrating. And her "last straw" at the employee holiday party was probably long overdue, given Ted's anxious attachment style. Is it any wonder she felt relieved when the relationship ended?

For many of us who confuse love with obsession, there is a destructive tendency to verbally strike out against a partner whenever we become fearful of infidelity and abandonment, oftentimes without cause. It is important to examine the cause of these fears and understand why they appear in our various relationships.

Sam

SITUATION: Stalked by a local media personality

Age: thirty-one. Successful entrepreneur.

I used to see Claudette on the morning news show each weekday doing the "culture beat" segment of the program. To watch her on the television set and to hear her voice, you would think she was a goddess of kindness and beauty, but let me tell you—appearances can be deceiving. As fate would have it, we ended up bumping into one another one evening when I was attending an AIDS fund-raiser at a local art gallery. Her station had sent her there to cover the event as part of

its public service requirement with the Federal Communications Commission. Because I was one of the event spon-
sors, she interviewed me "live" to talk about the cause. I was
extremely attracted to her, so when she finished covering the
event, I made it a point of telling her that she was even more
beautiful in person than she was on TV. She apparently liked
me too, because she ended up coming over to my house later
that evening and sleeping with me. One thing led to another,
and pretty soon we started dating. But like I said, looks can be
deceiving.

After just six months of being together, Claudette started
acting like a maniac. She would call me late at night on the
phone just to see if I picked up. God help me if I didn't answer because she would rush over to my house to check up on
me. Want to talk about annoying! Then during the day when
I was at work, she would call six or ten times within the
course of a few hours to find out what I was doing. In fact,
there were some mornings I would walk into my office and
the phone would be ringing off the hook, with my secretary
saying, "Something is wrong with that girl; she is one sick
puppy." And the other thing she did, for some reason, was
ask, "Do you still love me?" It ended up that I would have
to tell her "I do" at least three to four times a day just to
keep her mouth shut. It was like she was trying to force love,
you know?

She also started going through my stuff, checking to see
if I had telephone numbers. She found an old love letter
from my ex-girlfriend and became enraged. She would say
things like, "Do you still love that bitch? If you don't, why did
you keep her note?" I felt so violated when she did that and
so helpless. It was as if she had her mind made up about my
intentions before I even got a word out. Then she decided to
start spreading rumors about me to all of my former girl-

friends, telling them I had STDs and for them to go get tested. Talk about a bitch! It wasn't like I was cheating on her or anything, because every free moment of my time was spent with Claudette firmly planted up my rear end. I lost all of my friends because she attached herself to me like "white on rice." Still, I liked her and was hoping we could work things out, but I soon realized this was not possible.

One night while watching a ball game at home, I heard my home security perimeter alarm go off. It seemed odd, because in order for that to go off, someone would have had to scale an eight-foot-high concrete wall that surrounded my property because the gates to the driveway were shut and locked. It didn't take long to figure out who the intruder was. From my patio I heard someone pounding so loudly on the glass that I thought it was going to break. As I made my way toward all of the commotion and in between poundings, I heard a female voice screaming, "Open it up now because I know *she* is with you!" When I unlocked the door and opened it, Claudette ran right past me, charging into my home and looking around for the "other woman." I can only imagine how embarrassed she was to discover that I had been home sick with the flu. Somehow, she had gotten it into her head that I was cheating on her when I didn't pick up the phone earlier that evening because I was bent over the toilet, puking my guts out. She ended up spending the night on the couch wanting to take care of me, despite my repeated requests for her to leave. I was too sick and too tired to argue with her.

The next morning over toast and coffee, I finally told her that I wanted to end the relationship. She *freaked!* In the days following the breakup, she harassed me at home and left threatening messages, telling me she would "expose me on TV" for business fraud. Other times, she would call and leave messages that said, "I love you—don't do this to us." If that weren't bad enough, she would drive around my home in her car, circling the block for hours to see what I was up to. The only way I could get her to stop was by having my attorney obtain a restraining order. Claudette might have been pretty, but she was a serious head case.

Sam and Claudette's Relationship

One can only imagine how Sam must have felt during the height of Claudette's uncontrollable, obsessive outbursts. That he reported feeling violated was perfectly understandable, given the abuse he endured. And his portrayal of her behaviors, in which he described her as a "head case," was actually the unintentional characterization of a person deeply immersed in the third phase of ORP.

Tragically, Sam's once strong feelings of attraction for Claudette and his genuine concern for her were erased by her unbearable, obsessive behaviors. In many ways, he must have felt like he was being hunted, much like an animal. She systematically harassed him several times per day on the telephone, stopped by his home unannounced, rifled through his personal belongings, and spread vicious rumors about him to former lovers. As if that were not bad enough, she trespassed on his private property and then stormed into his home in search of the phantom other woman, and when asked to leave, refused. In fact, the only way he could extract Claudette from his life was to obtain a restraining order.

Sam's perception of Claudette's behavior was partially correct when he said, "It was like she was trying to force love." Upon closer analysis, however, what Claudette was actually trying to obtain from him was validation, which is often confused with love by the relationally addicted. The following metaphorical story sheds some light on why Claudette, and others who are relationally addicted, act as they do.

Imagine a horse that, in search of water, stumbles across a drinking well and begins to quench its thirst. The more it drinks, however, the thirstier it becomes until, eventually, the well goes dry. Unable to comprehend what has happened, it keeps returning, trying to obtain what the well can no longer give. But what else could it do? It was the only place the horse knew to go to survive.

Frank

SITUATION: Single after a one-year relationship

Age: thirty-four. Bartender at a sports pub.

No doubt about it, Bobbie was *hot.* We met one evening when she walked into my bar looking for a pay phone after blowing a tire on the way back from her girlfriend's home. I was a little drunk after drinking shots with customers all night and, if the truth be known, pretty horny too. It was about one-thirty in the morning, and since it was near closing time, I offered to change her tire. While closing out my register, we made some small talk, and I learned that she was thirty years old and employed as a secretary for a law firm. She also told me that she had broken up with a guy named Derrick a few months earlier. I could tell that she liked me because through-out our conversation, she kept throwing me smiles and mak-ing a lot of eye contact. Well, when we got into my truck to drive over to her stranded hatchback, she grabbed my hand and started caressing it. I should have known right then and there that she was trouble. When I finished putting on her spare tire, we exchanged telephone numbers and called it a night.

The next evening, she came into my bar again and told me that she was really attracted to me and that she wanted to get to know me better. Looking back, it seemed sort of strange that she would have troubled herself to come into the bar when she could have easily called me on the phone. But because I was ignorant of her ways at this point, I told her that I was attracted to her too. So we set up a date for the next evening, agreeing to meet at her apartment and then head out to supper later on. As it turned out, we didn't end up going anywhere; instead we sat around and talked all night and had sex until the wee hours of the morning. I guess that is when the relationship started because we started seeing one another exclusively shortly afterward.

But after a year of dating, I began to get annoyed with her. She would appear in the bar at night and sit on a stool, wanting to talk and keep an eye on me. Whenever some of the female customers came in to order a drink and make small talk, she would get jealous and storm out of the bar, slamming the door behind her as she walked out. She never seemed to understand that part of being a bartender means talking to people; that's how you make your tips. It made me feel uncomfortable, so I asked her to not come in anymore. Of course, that is when the fights started, because she naturally assumed that I was cheating on her. She started refusing to have sex with me and would give me the silent treatment for days. Then she tried to get me to quit that job, and of course, I refused. I had already paid over a thousand dollars for bartending school and wasn't about to give up doing something that I loved. It was all so unhealthy. We would fight, have really hot sex, make up, and then fight again.

I decided to end the relationship when I found out from one of my customers that she was camping outside of the bar at night and watching me through one of the bar windows. Between all of our fights, her accusations, interrogations, and stalking, I had had my fill of Bobbie. So I walked out to her car and told her straight out, "It's over!" She got pissed off and ran after me into the bar and made a huge scene. I ended up having to have another guy cover for me so I could get her the hell out of there. But I held my guns when we got outside and let her know that we were through. But she refused to listen. She kept saying, "I love you, and I won't do it again." I wanted to believe her, but we had gone through this so many times that I knew she would never change.

For days after our breakup, she called my home and left really bizarre messages. On one of them, she said that she was going to kill herself because she was so depressed. I ended up calling her back because I was concerned that she might have been serious. After we talked on the phone for a while, I went over to her house to check up on her. When I walked in, she was sitting on the couch and appeared really out of it. She told me that she had no energy and had not eaten for days. On the table, I saw an empty bottle of vodka and half a dozen letters she had written to me, one of which was a suicide note. She was in bad shape and I was worried about her, so I suggested she get some help. Bobbie must have been living in a fantasy world or really drunk because she kept saying to me, "So are you done punishing me now?" and "How can we put this back together?" I had to leave because it was obvious to me that I was doing her more harm than good by being there. By the time I got home, she had left me seven messages begging me to come back to her house. In one of those messages she said, "I can see your face everywhere I turn, and I can't stand it!" I ended up having to change my telephone number because she would call daily and tell me that she could not stop thinking about me. Months after the whole ordeal, I discovered from a friend of mine that her ex-boyfriend, Derrick, had gone through the same thing with her. I hope she got some help because Bobbie had some real problems.

Frank and Bobbie's Relationship

Frank's emotional roller-coaster ride with Bobbie represents the frustrations of what so many of our partners endure as they try to make sense of our obsessive, controlling behaviors. To Frank's credit, he stayed in the relationship as long as he could but ultimately had to let it go when Bobbie lost self-control. His relational communication style, which was more laid back and easygoing, was simply incompatible with her disease process. The more he tried to reason with her, the more suspicious she became. The more he tried to distance himself from her because of her outbursts, the more rejected she felt. When her loss of self-control culminated in stalking behaviors, Frank had no choice but to sever ties. After he ended the relationship, Bobbie immediately plunged into phase four of ORP, a phase that he was totally incapable of helping her deal with. Although we cannot be sure, the empty bottle of vodka lends clues to a possible drinking problem, which may have become exacerbated after the breakup. To gain further insight, let's examine the relationship in more detail.

On the night Frank and Bobbie met, Frank galloped into Bobbie's life and majestically rescued her from distress. But he unknowingly rescued her from something else that evening—*herself.* For some people who confuse love with obsession, being romantically involved with another person is required to function normally. At the time she and Frank crossed paths, she was no doubt experiencing the final phase of ORP after the collapse of her relationship with Derrick. In order to pass through this phase, she needed to attach herself to someone new, which ultimately set the Obsessive Love Wheel back to the attraction phase. The manner in which she related to men and her style of attachment to them was no doubt a cyclical pattern that she had probably repeated many times over the course of her life.

The following story illustrates how a relationally addicted person cannot avoid this inevitable road to disaster.

Imagine you are driving your car down a country road on a lazy summer day and see dark, ominous storm clouds gathering on the horizon. As lightning streaks across the sky and high winds push your car back and forth, you suddenly notice a funnel cloud rapidly heading in your direction. Although your instincts tell you to turn the car around, you are unable to do so. Instead, your foot punches on the accelerator, causing you to speed off toward disaster. Saving yourself *might* be possible but only if you can find another country road.

If you experienced discomfort, frustration, or embarrassment while reading about the various people in this chapter, or for that matter any person in this book, it is because this person's silent pain mirrored some part of your past. In fact, pain is what this addiction of relational dependency is all about.

In many ways, our addiction to another causes us to become prisoners within our own minds, sentencing us to a lifetime of cruel, self-inflicted abuse with each new relationship. Which brings us to the central questions of this chapter: How did we manage to find the people whom we became addicted to? And equally important, what is so special about them that causes us to become obsessed? If we accept the premise that nothing happens in the universe randomly, then it stands to reason that there is a reason why we cross paths with someone at a particular point in our life and, ultimately, become addicted to this person. In many ways, the object of our obsession represents a repressed need that is beyond our level of awareness. Within the first few minutes of meeting this special person, something unexplainable happens that causes a spark of what *was* from our childhood and a spark of what *might be* from our adulthood to combine and ignite, setting off a fire of love within our hearts so bright that it becomes blinding. We are drawn to the fire's light because it warms us and seems to fill a void deep within our hidden selves, making us feel whole.

Simply put, the way we love is learned. Our unhealthy attachments to others are a result of the damages that were inflicted on us as children. In fact, our past has had such a profound effect on why and whom we love that it becomes the driving force behind our styles of attachment. And more often than not, our styles of relating to others and the way we express our love is destructive.

For those of us who confuse love with obsession, destruction is indeed the end result of many of our relationships, as we hopelessly try to hold on to that which is no more. It is for this reason that the Obsessive Love Wheel is characterized as painful, for as we pass through the various phases of our obsessive relationships, we unintentionally inflict great harm on others and ourselves. Fueled by isolation and a need to be needed, our wheel spins with increasing velocity, turning faster and faster until it takes on a chaotic life of its own. As we ride the wheel on its path to destruction, we sink deeper and deeper into an abyss of obsession that eventually overtakes everything that once held importance in our lives. Nothing matters when we are on the wheel, including our jobs, our families, our friends, or our sense of self. For many of us, the only way to "move on" is to start a new relationship, repeating the painful cycle that we have come to know all too well—and for many more of us, one that has become a way of life.

It doesn't have to be this way. Loving another person *does not* have to mean living in agony. Sharing your life with someone *does not* have to mean being in control. If you have the courage to end the cycle of destruction in your life—to embark down a path where peace replaces chaos and tears of pain transform into gentle mists of harmony—proceed to the following chapter, which offers a chance at recovery.

8

FINDING YOU—
A PATH TO RECOVERY

Love always creates. It never destroys.
In this lies man's only promise.

—Leo Buscaglia

NOTICE I DID NOT TITLE THIS CHAPTER "*The* Path to Recovery." You see, each of us must find our own unique way to healing. Unfortunately, there is no quick-fix, one-size-fits-all type of treatment for the disease of relational dependency. Individual life events, personal situations, and childhood traumas must all be considered as part of any treatment program. That is why "finding you" is such an important component on our individual paths to recovery.

As persons who confuse love with obsession, we have endured horrific emotional damage over the course of our lifetimes, some of it beyond our level of awareness. It is this damage, this pain that we must discover and acknowledge in order for the healing process to begin. Our addiction has caused so many of us to lose sight of who we are as individuals, because we have become so wrapped up in *them*, the objects of our affection. Everything we are and everything we want to be is lost in that violent, never-ending storm of relational dependency. Finding who we are allows us to see who we need to be.

Now, however, we have seen our unhealthy patterns through the experiences of others who believed that being in love meant being in control. We have seen how manipulation, psychological violence, behavioral self-policing, money, alcohol, other drugs, food, sex, and many other devices can be used as tools of control to keep another attached to a relationship. We need to ask ourselves: Is this really love?

And so here we are at the crossroads; we can either continue down the same path that we know all too well, *or* we can take the first steps toward someplace new. As with anything in life, unfamiliarity brings about anxiety. However, we should be comforted in knowing that if we choose to take a different path, we will discover something that has long been forgotten—ourselves. Don't we owe it to ourselves to at least try?

What follows are some basic steps, or guidelines, that others have found to be beneficial on their own paths to recovery. Although these steps are listed numerically, it is not necessary to complete them in the order that they appear; it is important, though, to complete them all. Again, each of us must find our own path to healing and pressuring ourselves should not be part of the process. I have placed an asterisk next to certain steps that others have found to be most helpful when completed first.

1. Forgive yourself.
2. Forgive those who have harmed you.
3. Uncover the relationship role you have adopted.
4. Be honest about any coaddictions.
5. Locate a trained professional.*
6. Join a support group.*
7. Consider tapping into a Higher Power.
8. Identify your tools of control.

9. Invest in yourself.
10. Love yourself.

These steps will not be easy to complete; each requires an ongoing, personal commitment coupled with a new way of thinking. Remember, it has taken a lifetime to become a person who confuses love with obsession, and we cannot expect to heal overnight. We can, however, begin the *process* of healing by using these steps as part of our recovery plan.

Let's review each of these guidelines in detail, placing special emphasis on the importance of each step. Included in each step are suggestions and exercises (some of which can be completed mentally) to support our recovery with the ultimate goal of "finding you."

STEP ONE: FORGIVE YOURSELF

The Importance of Self-Forgiveness

Forgiving yourself means not blaming yourself for the things that you have done to others in the past. It also means not beating yourself up for self-inflicted harms. The disease of relational dependency causes you to act out in ways that are often beyond your ability to control. So much of the unexplained anger you experience emanates from repressed feelings of self-hatred that make you lash out against others. Forgiving yourself is important because it frees you from self-slavery, meaning you no longer have to be a prisoner of your own mind. Part of the reason you fall so deeply into depressive states is because of the guilt you feel for harming others, both conscious and subconscious. The importance of forgiving yourself cannot be overstated, because it is necessary in order to get past the shame of your illness.

Nobody chooses to be a relationship addict, including you. For reasons beyond your control, you developed unhealthy attachments to others that caused you to engage in behaviors that, to most people, are unacceptable. *All* of us are imperfect beings, capable of doing terrible things to one another. A person is not defined solely by one feature or characteristic, such as gender, job title, or for that matter, addiction. So you should *never* let anyone define you by your mistakes. To understand this better, ask yourself this question: If a relationally addicted man throws a rock through his ex-wife's window during the height of his illness, does that mean that for the rest of his life he should be thought of as a criminal?

Try to remember that the past may make up *part* of who you are, but it does not make up the *whole* of who you are. Once you have forgiven yourself for those less-than-flattering aspects of your past, including the harms you have done to others and yourself, something liberating happens. All of the repressed anger that you have kept locked inside for so long begins to evaporate, allowing the light of harmony to illuminate the dark parts of your hidden self. Power that others have over you occurs only when you give it to them. In short, you can end the cycle of self-hatred by learning to forgive yourself.

Ways to Find Yourself through Self-Forgiveness

Achieving self-forgiveness involves acknowledging the harmful actions you have taken against others and yourself. This is not easy, because it will force you to come face-to-face with some rather unpleasant reminders of your addiction. However, once you have acknowledged your past actions, you can be free of them.

Consider the following exercise as part of a self-forgiveness ritual with the goal of "finding you." Repeat this as often as necessary.

- Write down all of the things that you are mad at yourself about, including any mistakes that you have made in the past. If you find that you are unable to do this in one sitting, that's okay. There is no time rule with this exercise. The purpose of this ritual is to recall those things that you have repressed and take ownership for what you may have denied. If it takes you thirty days and fifty sheets of paper to write it all down, so be it. When you have finished writing down your thoughts, consider doing one of the following items as part of a cleansing process.
- Light a candle and meditate on what you have written. During this process, allow yourself to feel whatever emotions bubble to the surface. When you feel satisfied that you have spent sufficient time engaging in this activity, blow the candle out and throw the papers away.
- Gather all of the papers you have written your thoughts on and place them in an envelope. On the envelope, use a marker to write: *The Past*. Then take the envelope and place it in a spot where you will see it. After you feel enough time has passed, choose one piece of paper to represent all that are in the envelope. Tie it to a balloon. Set the balloon free. As it floats away, allow yourself to feel the anger leaving your body.
- Write a letter to yourself listing all of the reasons why it's important for you to practice the act of self-forgiveness. Beneath the letter, place the sheets of paper containing your thoughts. Then take all of the papers and put them in a bowl of water, allowing the ink to run off the pages until you have nothing left but white sheets.

STEP TWO: FORGIVE THOSE WHO HAVE HARMED YOU

The Importance of Forgiving Others

If your first thought upon reading this step was "easier said than done," you are right. Forgiving those who have harmed you involves recalling the specific grievances you have against an individual, such as a parent or partner. It also involves validating your pain. By no means does this step mean "getting over it." As I said in the introduction, only a fool thinks that it is possible to wave a magic wand and make pain disappear. When we love deeply, we hurt deeply. Your pain runs so deep because someone *you* loved hurt *you*.

Perhaps the most difficult pain to come to terms with is the pain that was inflicted by a parent. This problem becomes compounded if either one or both of your parents have died and you can no longer address your grievances directly. To be sure, there is a sacred bond between a child and a parent that no words can truly describe. Childhood love for a mother or father is innate and powerfully influential. When that love is violated by psychological, physical, emotional, and/or sexual abuse, it rips away an innocence that can never be replaced. And when your parents have emotionally abandoned you, it drives a stake through the very heart of your hidden self. Is it really that surprising that you have had a fear of abandonment in your personal relationships?

Pain that a partner (former or current) inflicts on you can be equally painful. Unfortunately, you sometimes choose to love people who are unhealthy for you, but only because you are relating to that which is familiar. (Is it any wonder why so many of us who confuse love with obsession have involved ourselves with abusive partners over the course of our lives?) However, regardless of how unhealthy that person was (or is) for you, you still cared for him. When those feelings are violated, it hurts deeply.

To forgive those who have harmed you, you must first recognize that anger is not necessarily a bad thing. Society teaches us that feelings such as jealousy, anger, pain, and resentment are unhealthy emotions and must be quickly done away with. This is simply not true. Feelings are neither good nor bad, they just *are*. In fact, without these feelings, you would be unable to appreciate the magnificence of the human experience. Think of these feelings as teachers rather than as something negative. Ask yourself: What can be learned from my pain?

It is what you do with your pain that matters. Part of forgiving those who have harmed you means acknowledging the anger inside and understanding why it exists. It means recognizing that you have a right to feel hurt and that what happened to you was wrong. But most important, it means forgiving another unconditionally. In other words, you should not set up barriers (e.g., I will forgive Dad once he tells me he is sorry). Why is this point important? Because setting up barriers will rob you of the chance of healing. By learning to validate your feelings and understanding why they exist, you will be in a better position to set them free. Once this happens, you will be able to transform your hurt into something more useful—hope for the future.

Ways to Find Yourself through Forgiving Others

That you hurt deeply means that you loved deeply. Forgiving another person for the harms inflicted on you is not easy. The expectations you have of a loved one are fragile, and when those expectations are violated, you experience pain. Once you are able to let go of that pain, you are able to empty your heart of hurt and replace it with self-love.

Consider doing the following exercises when forgiving those who have harmed you. Repeat these exercises as often as necessary.

- Journal your feelings about the anger you have against those who have hurt you. Do not restrict yourself by following a self-imposed format. Write down whatever comes to mind, no matter how bizarre it may seem. If you have to walk away from what you are writing because you are experiencing pain or are overwhelmed by emotion, that is okay. You are doing this project to find yourself, and the process is not easy. If you want to share your letter with someone supportive (e.g., your therapist or group support sponsor), do so. (See steps five and six for more information on therapy and support groups.)
- Write a letter to the one who harmed you, but *don't* mail it. In your letter, let this person know how her behavior (e.g., neglect or physical abuse) hurt you. If the person is no longer living, the exercise will still have meaning. Once again, if you choose to, you can share your letter with a supportive person.

STEP THREE: UNCOVER THE RELATIONSHIP ROLE YOU HAVE ADOPTED

The Importance of Uncovering Your Relationship Role

The way you relate to others is directly linked to your past. For many reasons that were beyond your control, you adopted a certain role in your childhood that became imprinted on your hidden self. Uncovering this role will help you understand why you relate to romantic partners the way that you do. In this book, it is not possible to list every role that relationally dependent people adopt in their relationships. However, identifying your specific relational role is important in order to begin the process of self-analysis. Some of the roles listed below are taken from Jean Kinney's seventh edition of the book *Loosening the Grip: A Handbook of Alcohol Information*.

If you grew up in a chaotic environment where you were

forced to take care of others because a parent was unable to, it is only natural to take that adopted role and carry it into adulthood *(caretaker)*. If your parents constantly fought with one another, it was only natural for you to want to keep the peace *(peacemaker)*. If you felt family members rejected you through neglect or abuse, you may have engaged in angry, defiant behaviors to seek their attention *(scapegoat)*. If you went along with unhealthy behaviors at home, such as alcoholism or drug abuse, and/or even excused it, then you have enabled it *(enabler)*. If you withdrew from your family because of abuse and have become isolated, you became lost *(lost child)*.

As stated throughout this book, it is human nature to relate to that which is familiar. The way you love is indeed learned. Understanding the reasons why you are attracted to certain types of people and then identifying your particular role in a relationship helps you to see how certain associations with others may be harmful to you. It also helps you to understand how you have set yourself up for pain. Sometimes, children may adopt more than one role because they had to (which is normal).

By identifying the particular childhood role that you adopted from your youth, you can begin to change the way you relate to others in the here and now. This involves a certain degree of self-honesty, meaning that you must recognize and admit if you are in denial about any of the behaviors that go along with your particular role. Liberating yourself from this role will allow you to develop healthier approaches in your personal relationships. It will also allow you to see how others you are involved with may be perpetuating their own childhood roles.

True love is unselfish and does not have a mask. By freeing yourself of your childhood role, you will be able to experience the joy of self-love (we'll talk more about this in step ten).

Ways to Find Yourself through Uncovering
Your Relationship Role

The roles you adopted in your childhood have followed you into adulthood. These roles have caused you to become attracted to and enter into relationships with those who might be unhealthy for you. These roles have also caused you to engage in controlling behaviors against your partners, which, you now recognize, occurred through no fault of your own.

Uncovering your adopted childhood role will allow you to understand why you relate to romantic partners the way you do. It will also allow you to identify the specific behaviors involved with that particular role so you can stop doing them. Consider doing the following exercises as part of uncovering your adopted childhood role:

- Analyze the various relationships you have been involved with over the course of your lifetime. Search for any patterns that may exist (e.g., Have you always provided for the other person?).
- Spend some time with yourself and visualize your ideal partner. Then write down the reasons why you are attracted to this person. Allow yourself to imagine being in a relationship with your ideal mate and then ask yourself, "What role did I adopt and why?"
- Reflect on your past relationships and consider how your adopted childhood role may have influenced your behaviors. Then ask yourself, "How did my childhood role damage the relationship?" and "How did my childhood role damage me?"
- Consider the types of people you are attracted to and ask yourself, "If I were not able to act out my childhood role, would I have been attracted to this person in the first place?"

STEP FOUR: BE HONEST ABOUT ANY COADDICTIONS

The Importance of Being Honest about Coaddictions

For many who confuse love with obsession, it is common to struggle with a coaddiction. In order to cope with your pain (and to run from it), you have learned to medicate yourself with alcohol, other drugs, gambling, food, and sex. When the object of your affection causes you anxiety or hurts you, you turn to substances or unhealthy behaviors to numb the pain. If a relationship is forced to end, you compensate for your loss by escalating these coaddictive behaviors.

Part of recovering from relational dependency means being brutally honest about those unhealthy behaviors. Addictions to alcohol, other drugs, gambling, food, and sex are closely related to one another and are related to your obsessive behaviors in your relationships. Being honest about your coaddictions helps you understand why you engage in destructive behaviors against others and yourself. It is important to note that a dependency on a substance is part of an overall disease process, meaning that if left untreated, it is likely to cause harm and even death.

It is not possible to address all the various kinds of addictions in this book, or the related treatments. It is, however, possible to encourage you to be honest about an addiction you may have and to analyze how it is related to your need to be attached to and control another. Taking an honest look at coaddictions allows you to face your addiction to relationships with deeper clarity.

Ways to Find Yourself through Being Honest about Coaddictions

Acknowledging the existence of a coaddiction is an important step in your recovery from relational dependency. Part of being honest about other dependencies means not beating yourself up over having them. Self-blame does nothing more than wound your self-esteem and cause depression. Helping yourself break free of a coaddiction takes time. Consider doing the following as part of being honest about your coaddictions:

- Locate a trained professional (see step five).
- Join a support group for the coaddiction you suffer with (see "Appendix B: Resources for Help").

STEP FIVE: LOCATE A TRAINED PROFESSIONAL

The Importance of Locating a Trained Professional

The issues surrounding your dependency on another person run deep within your hidden self. The fact of the matter is this: The need to be attached to and control your partners is something you cannot deal with on your own. Talking to a professional trained to uncover what has made you become addicted to others helps put things in perspective. Trained professionals can include (but are not limited to) licensed clinical professional counselors, licensed clinical social workers, family and marriage therapists, psychologists, and psychiatrists. In your search for the right therapist, consider finding a person who comes from a cognitive-behavioral approach. *Cognitive-behavioral therapy* is a term used to describe work done with a therapist who is trained in disrupting unhealthy thought processes and in helping you to replace them with more productive ones.

For so long, you have tried to handle your obsessive behaviors on your own, only to be disappointed. Seeking the help of a therapist does not mean that you are crazy or weak or any of the other stereotypes that our culture has associated with counseling. You might be surprised to know that most people who provide therapy to others regularly attend therapy themselves. There is no shame in needing the support of a trained professional to help you understand the beautiful person you are. Sharing your secret pain with someone who understands your problem while acting as your personal advocate can be liberating.

The length of time you spend in therapy depends on a variety of issues, including the severity of your problems, your willingness to fully engage in the therapeutic process, and of course, your overall level of commitment to change. When you go to your first therapy session, be prepared to answer some basic questions about your background (to give the therapist further insight into your situation). Also, you may be asked to engage in various activities, depending on the goals you and your therapist have decided upon. Think of these activities as a chance for you to grow and heal. Believe it or not, you might even have fun. Remember, your therapist is your advocate, meaning he is not going to judge you. It is this person's job to help you understand who you *are* and who you *want to be.*

Something wonderful happens when you begin the therapeutic process with a trained professional. You begin to "find you."

Ways to Find Yourself through a Trained Professional

The pain that you have endured runs deep within your hidden self. Feelings, both conscious and subconscious, have a way of expressing themselves in unhealthy ways in your romantic relationships. Your need to obsess over and control another is closely linked to your past. Working with a trained professional will help you understand why you behave the way you do. The goal of therapy for the relationally dependent should be making the subconscious conscious.

Consider the following as part of "finding you" through a trained professional:

- Locate a trained professional who is knowledgeable about relational dependency. Some people who confuse love with obsession have called a therapist and asked if the helping professional is experienced with issues related to codependency. Also, if you find it easier to speak to a female professional as opposed to a male, then follow your intuition. If you identify yourself as gay, lesbian, or bisexual, you may want to see someone who is sensitive to your needs. Sources for finding a therapist include your phone book, the Internet, local newspapers, and of course, word of mouth. You can also call a crisis line for a referral. Don't be afraid to ask questions.

- If you suffer from other addictions, make sure the therapist has training with these issues as well.

- If cost is a problem, consider using the services of a community mental health center that has a sliding scale. Also, many employee insurance programs offer mental health services as part of an overall benefits package (most employers do not even know you are using this service).

- Be open to engaging in activities with your therapist that at first may seem strange. You may be asked to role-play or speak to your therapist as if she were a parent or significant other. Some therapists may ask you to sign a contract with yourself and set behavioral goals. Other therapists may provide you homework assignments to help encourage insight and self-growth. All of these activities are normal and will help you in the healing process.

STEP SIX: JOIN A SUPPORT GROUP

The Importance of Joining a Support Group

One of the most difficult and painful realities of relational dependency is experiencing extreme feelings of isolation. Letting others know about your addiction to relationships, including the behaviors you use to keep others attached to the relationship, makes you feel ashamed and embarrassed. At the heart of your concerns are powerful feelings of rejection and concerns about abandonment. When rejection has characterized most of your lifetime relationships, it is only natural to want to avoid that which might cause pain.

What's important for you to realize is *you are not alone.* In fact, many people struggle with an addiction to their relationships (and possibly other coaddictions as well). Recovery from relational dependency requires breaking free of your isolation and sharing your secret pain in a safe and supportive environment. People in support groups understand your silent pain because they have lived it. The first time I entered a support group for the relationally addicted, I was terrified. In time, however, my fears transformed into a sense of belonging because I began to identify with others who had the same problem I did. In time, I became a sponsor.

By allowing yourself to unite with others who have similar backgrounds, experiences, feelings, and struggles, you will begin to experience the joy of self-acceptance, which ultimately promotes self-love. Isolation need not be a way of life for you. Recovery from your addiction is possible when you begin to reach out and share your pain with others. More important, they will reach out to you.

Nothing you say in the group will be repeated because all conversations are strictly confidential. In fact, revealing that you (or someone else) are a member of a support group is prohibited (it is for this reason I have chosen not to identify which support group I was involved with).

So as part of your recovery plan and in cooperation with your therapist, join a support group. There is no need for you to carry the burden of your addiction by yourself. There are people who want to help you and who need your help.

Ways to Find Yourself through a Support Group

Your feelings of isolation have caused much pain in your life, leading to depression and low self-esteem. By understanding that there are many other people just like you who suffer from an addiction, you will be able to experience powerful feelings of belonging. There really is a difference between going through the motions of life and *living life*. By reaching out, you are really reaching in.

Consider the following as part of "finding you" when joining a support group:

- Choose a support group that addresses the issue of relational dependency. Use the "Resources for Help" section located in appendix B to help you identify such a group.
- If you suffer from a coaddiction, join a support group that addresses that particular problem. Again, use the "Resources for Help" section to identify a group.
- Allow yourself time to adjust to the group dynamics. In most support groups, there are certain guidelines that members adhere to in order for the group to function smoothly.
- Don't place pressure on yourself by thinking that you have to disclose your feelings right away. It is perfectly okay to sit and listen to others before making a contribution. When you feel comfortable, share what feels right.
- Be prepared to make a commitment, meaning that you

should plan on attending the support group at least once a week, but more if you can. Some people find it helpful to go every day initially. For example, it may be helpful to create a goal of attending ninety meetings in ninety days to build momentum in your recovery.

• Don't be afraid to sample different kinds of support groups. If you are more comfortable with a certain kind of group as opposed to another, use the one that makes you feel most comfortable.

STEP SEVEN: CONSIDER TAPPING INTO A HIGHER POWER

The Importance of Tapping into a Higher Power

For some, the term *Higher Power* conjures up all sorts of religious connotations. It is for this reason that many who confuse love with obsession reject using a Higher Power as part of a recovery program. However, tapping into a Higher Power does not mean that you have to join a church or subscribe to a certain definition of God. In fact, it is possible to tap into a Higher Power without believing in the concept of God at all. What it does mean is that you turn to sources of spirituality that have meaning to *you*. For example, some people identify their Higher Power as Jesus Christ. Others believe in God. And still others believe in certain spiritual principles, such as those presented in Buddhism.

Tapping into a Higher Power allows you to surrender your problems to another place, which gives you the peace of mind of not having to solve all of life's problems. A Higher Power fortifies you during moments when you want to give in to your addiction. It is a source of strength to turn to. During your quiet moments, when anxiety and fear engulf your every thought, your Higher Power can help you gain solace.

Ways to Find Yourself through a Higher Power

A Higher Power is a resource for you to turn to during life's difficult moments. But you can also turn to your Higher Power at other times. Thanking your Higher Power for what's good in your life helps you focus on the positive while changing your thought processes, which can often be self-defeating. The more you turn to your Higher Power, the more empowered you become. Part of using a Higher Power means getting in touch with your spirituality.

Consider doing the following exercises when "finding you" through the use of a Higher Power. Repeat these exercises as often as necessary.

- Reflect upon what a Higher Power means to you. When you have given sufficient thought to this meaning, write a letter to your Higher Power and release your worries.
- Review the affirmations listed in appendix A of this book. If you see an affirmation that has a special meaning to you, write it down and hang it up where you will see it.
- Write your own affirmation and repeat it to yourself whenever you feel the need. If you want, share your affirmation with your therapist or people in your support group.

STEP EIGHT: IDENTIFY YOUR TOOLS OF CONTROL

The Importance of Identifying Your Tools of Control

Being honest about your addiction to relationships means identifying the various tools of control you use to keep another attached to the relationship. Manipulating another person to behave the way you want does not happen on its own. When you confuse love with obsession, you fall victim to giving in to your anxieties and using various mechanisms to exert control over the people you love.

In order to heal from your addiction, you must analyze

which tools of control you use. This can be particularly painful if you have caused harm to those whom you have loved. This, however, is a necessary step if you wish to make recovery a priority in your life. This step will not be easy. In fact, naming your tools of control may be one of the hardest things you will ever do in your life. This may be difficult because it will force you to confront your actions.

Regret, self-blame, and denial are to be expected when confronting the unpleasant side of your addiction and are quite normal to feel. By identifying your tools of control, you will begin the process of understanding why you use them. Understanding why you use a particular tool ultimately will lead to its demise.

Let me provide you with an example to illustrate this point: One of the people in my support group revealed that she used emotions as a tool of control to keep her partner attached to the relationship. By withholding her emotions, she was able to play mind games with her partner and get him to show her the attention she wanted. With the help of her therapist, she later discovered that she used this tool because as a child, she withdrew from her family and found withholding emotions was an effective means of gaining attention (a classic example of the lost child role).

Do you now see why it is important to identify your adopted childhood role and the tools of control you use in your romantic relationships?

Ways to Find Yourself through Your Tools of Control

Discovering your tools of control means spending time examining your behaviors. This is not easy, because it will require that you make a commitment to self-honesty. If recovery is ever to be achieved, however, identifying your tools of control must be included in the healing process.

Consider doing the following exercises as part of "finding

you" through identifying your tools of control. Repeat as often as necessary.

- Find a quiet place in your home and reflect on your current and/or past relationships. During your quiet time, meditate on the various means you used to manipulate a partner into behaving the way you wanted. Ask yourself, "What tool did I use?" Do not become alarmed if you see yourself using more than one tool, as this is quite common. When you feel satisfied that you have spent sufficient time on this activity, record your findings on a piece of paper. Consider sharing this with your therapist or someone in your support group.
- Draw a circle on a piece of paper with a line through the center of it. On one side of the circle, write down the name of a partner you have manipulated. On the other side of the circle, write down whatever comes to your mind as it relates to manipulating this person. When you are finished, circle anything that might be used as a tool of control and meditate on it. Record your findings on a piece of paper and share it with your therapist or someone from your support group.
- Listen to people in your support group and reflect on what they have revealed. If they discuss a manipulative behavior that mirrors something you have done (or are doing) in a relationship, ask yourself, "Am I using this behavior as a tool of control?"

STEP NINE: INVEST IN YOURSELF

The Importance of Investing in Yourself

The tragic reality for you, because of your addiction, is that you have become a stranger to yourself. This happens when you focus all of your energy on the objects of your affection, with the goal of manipulating them into behaving in ways that you want. This also happens when you obsess about *their* feelings, *their* needs, and, ultimately, *their* happiness, while woefully neglecting your own. Simply put, when you can't stop controlling your partner and the relationship, you can't cultivate the most important relationship of all—a relationship with yourself.

Investing in you is perhaps one of the most important parts of your recovery plan. This is because the disease of relational dependency does much damage to your self-esteem. Somewhere along the line, you began to believe that validating yourself could be accomplished through associations with romantic partners. You began to confuse the term *I* with *us* and *me* with *we*.

In order to change this misguided way of thinking and to begin the recovery process, you must begin to get in touch with who you are. To be blunt, you must begin to rebuild your self-esteem and self-worth so you will not be dependent on another for your happiness. This is easier said than done. It requires spending time with yourself and engaging in healthy activities. For some, the thought of doing this is terrifying. This is understandable if you have suffered from a deeply held fear of abandonment and have attached yourself to another in order to not feel alone. But if you want to stop the anxious behaviors, if you want to stop the obsessing, if you want to stop the controlling, then you must work on linking your personal happiness to a relationship with yourself and not to a relationship with another. Aren't you tired of cycling through all of the destructive relationships anyway? Aren't you ready to get off of that Obsessive Love Wheel and start attending to your needs?

Once you begin to look inward for happiness rather than to the outside, a whole new life opens up for you. All of the energy you have directed toward controlling your relationships will become redirected toward more important things, such as engaging in activities that help you grow as a person. Your self-esteem will begin to blossom, and your need to be needed by another will transform into another kind of a need—a need to be needed by you.

Ways to Find Yourself through Investing in Yourself

Building your self-esteem is important to your recovery. Free of your need to be needed, you will begin to value who you are, rather than who you are with. Once you accomplish this, the way you relate to others will be forever changed.

Consider doing the following exercises as part of "finding you" through fostering a relationship with yourself. Repeat any of these as needed.

- Take a piece of paper and draw a line down the middle of it. Title the right side "What life goals have I given up because of my addiction to (fill in the name of the person you are addicted to)." Title the left side "How I plan on investing in myself to realize these goals." On the bottom of the paper, write: "For the next thirty days, I, (fill in your name), will invest in myself by working on those things I have listed in my self-investment plan." When you have finished this project, sign the paper and place it somewhere that you will see. Each day that you do something to help yourself realize your goal, treat yourself to something pleasing (and healthy). At the end of the thirty days, reevaluate your progress and make adjustments as necessary. Your final reward will be when you have realized your goal (not to mention a huge boost to your self-esteem).
- Pretend you are writing your dream biography for the back of a book. What would you like others to know about you?

What makes you special? Now ask yourself, "How can I make this dream biography come true?"

- Write down at least three of your talents. Of these three, circle the one that is most appealing to you. Below your talents, number a list from one to ten. Next to each number, write down one thing you can do to build upon that talent (e.g., if you are good at cooking, you may want to consider taking a cooking class—but not because you want to cook better food for your partner!). At least once a week, pull out your list and ask yourself, "What have I done to help build upon my talent?"

- Spend one evening treating yourself (and no one else) to something you enjoy. Ideas might include listening to your favorite music or watching a special movie. At the end of your experience, write down how it felt to spend time alone. Ask yourself, "How did this help me grow as a person?" Also ask yourself, "How did I feel experiencing this alone? What can I do in the future on my own that might bring me enjoyment?"

- Pretend you have a time machine that can transport you to any date in the future. Mentally allow yourself to travel in your time machine to a future date of your choosing. Once you arrive, take a few moments to consider your surroundings, including your home, the people around you, and whatever else that you might desire. In other words, imagine that you are living the life of your financial, spiritual, and relational dreams. While you are there, take a pen and paper and write a letter to yourself. Outline the steps you took to reach your life goals and what you had to work on in order to achieve your dreams. When you are done with the letter, address it to yourself and put it in an envelope. Every so often, open the letter as a reminder of the self-investment goals you are working toward.

STEP TEN: LOVE YOURSELF

The Importance of Self-Love

This particular step must not be dismissed as a tired, self-help cliché. In fact, for the relationally dependent, it has special meaning. Perhaps the best way to put this into perspective is by asking the following question: If you have been loving others in unhealthy and destructive ways, then how healthy is the love you have for yourself? This leads to the next question: What does loving yourself really mean?

Loving yourself means making *you* the most important person in the world—more important than *his* next job interview, more important than *her* feelings, and more important than *their* livelihood. It means not placing all of your hopes and dreams into a relationship with *her*. It means not believing *him* when he tells you that he won't hit you again. It means not losing your job because you are too consumed with anxiety over *her* whereabouts. It means not having to suffer through another bout of diarrhea because you're afraid *he* is cheating on you. It means not losing another night's sleep because you can't get *her* out of your mind. It means not being a slave to the telephone waiting for *him* to call. It means not having another restraining order delivered to your doorstep. It means not using food, sex, emotions, money, or children to manipulate. It means not escalating your drinking or sexual activity because the relationship has collapsed. Quite simply, loving yourself means stopping all of the craziness in your life.

The only way to put an end to these unhealthy behaviors is to make the conscious decision that you no longer want to live your life this way and then doing what it takes to make it a reality. It means committing yourself to a path of recovery and then making it the focus of your daily life. It means talking to others about the disease of relational dependency and educating them about a problem that truly does not get better over time without help. It means offering support to others who suffer from this disease and sharing educational resources. It means looking inward to your hidden self and confronting the demons of your past. Finally, it means taking care of your emotional, physical, and spiritual health so that you are strong enough to know the difference between a healthy relationship and a destructive one.

Ways to Find Yourself through Self-Love

Self-love is the light that will illuminate your recovery. By putting your emotional, physical, and spiritual health ahead of all other priorities in your life, including your relationships, you will begin to heal and grow. By educating others about your disease, you will become stronger. By learning to give of yourself without the expectation of something in return, you will be giving to the most important person of all—you.

Consider doing the following as part of loving yourself:

- If you are a woman, consider doing some volunteer work at a battered women's shelter. If you are a man, consider volunteering your time at a food pantry.
- Educate your doctor about the disease of relational dependency and offer to bring some brochures from your support group.
- Unite with others who are addicted to their relationships and plan a community outreach event.
- Tell your sponsor and other support group members if you have slipped and accept their love.
- Use the "Resources for Help" section of this book to link others who suffer from addictions with assistance.

By giving of yourself, you will begin to truly love yourself. And together, we can lift our collective pain and truly seek shelter from the storm of relational dependency.

It is my sincere hope that this book has illuminated the unspeakable pain of millions of people around the world who suffer from a disease that is widely misunderstood and often undetected. If this is the case, then our tears of sorrow will have truly transformed into gentle mists of healing harmony.

Be well.

Appendix A
POSITIVE SELF-TALK

ENGAGING IN POSITIVE SELF-TALK reverses the negative effects of the hidden self. It quells fears and gives you strength to overcome the storm of relational dependency. In short, changing the way you view yourself changes *you*.

Consider saying the following several times each day as part of a recovery program:

I am a fortress of strength.
I am harmony and peace.
I have achieved happiness in my life because I have made it so.
My power comes from within.

I love myself because I know myself.
I am transforming every day into a new person.
Nothing can stop me from realizing my goals.

Peace and solitude are my reality.
Calmness and serenity accompany me wherever I go.
Tranquility and harmony flow within my hidden self.

Joy and happiness fuel my spirit.
The wings of light raise me up.
I can touch the sun with my soul.

When I see me, I love me.
My words are filled with happiness.
I can do anything I set my mind to.

Perhaps saying a prayer to your Higher Power works better for you as opposed to positive self-talk. If this is the case, include it in your recovery program. Here is a prayer from St. Francis you may want to consider:

Lord, make me an instrument of your peace.
Where there is hatred, let me sow love;
Where there is injury, pardon;
Where there is doubt, faith;
Where there is despair, hope;
Where there is darkness, light;
Where there is sadness, joy.

O divine Master, grant that I may not so much seek
To be consoled as to console,
To be understood as to understand,
To be loved as to love;
For it is in giving that we receive;
It is in pardoning that we are pardoned;
It is in dying to self that we are born to eternal life.

Meaningful positive self-talk is most meaningful when you create it. Use words that raise you up and empower you, that praise you, that *love* you. Why not give it a try?

Appendix B
RESOURCES FOR HELP

REACHING OUT TO OTHERS FOR HELP can sometimes be a daunting task. Because you may be dealing with a variety of personal issues, you may not even know where to start looking for assistance. One source to consider when you begin your search is your local social services agency. When you call, ask to speak to a case manager or social worker and be honest about the kind of help you want to receive. If you are concerned about anonymity, don't be. You can share with them as much or as little information as you like; you don't even have to give your name. Social service agencies often provide counseling services and can link you to an appropriate group.

You can also use the Internet to conduct your search for help. And be sure to consider contacting some of the following agencies to learn more about their services:

Alcoholics Anonymous (AA)
General Service Office
P.O. Box 459
New York, NY 10163
Tel: (212) 870-3400
Web: www.aa.org

Cocaine Anonymous World Services (CA)
3740 Overland Avenue, Suite C
Los Angeles, CA 90034
Tel: (310) 559-5833
Web: www.ca.org

Co-Dependents Anonymous (CoDA)
P.O. Box 33577
Phoenix, AZ 85067-3577
Web: www.codependents.org

Debtors Anonymous (DA)
General Service Office
P.O. Box 920888
Needham, MA 02492-0009
Tel: (781) 453-2743
Web: www.debtorsanonymous.org

Incest Survivors Anonymous (ISA)
P.O. Box 17245
Long Beach, CA 90807-7245
Tel: (562) 428-5599
Web: www.lafn.org/medical/isa/home.html

LAMBDA GBLT Community Services
Anti-Violence Project
216 South Ochoa Street
El Paso, TX 79901
Tel: (206) 350-4283
Web: www.lambda.org

Narcotics Anonymous World Services (NA)
P.O. Box 9999
Van Nuys, CA 91409
Tel: (818) 773-9999
Web: www.na.org

National Coalition Against Domestic Violence (NCADV)
1120 Lincoln Street, Suite 1603
Denver, CO 80203
Tel: (303) 839-1852
Web: www.ncadv.org

National Suicide Prevention Lifeline
Tel: (800) 273-TALK (800-273-8255)
Web: www.suicidepreventionlifeline.org

Overeaters Anonymous (OA)
World Service Office
P.O. Box 44020
Rio Rancho, NM 87174-4020
Tel: (505) 891-2664
Web: www.overeatersanonymous.org

Recovering Couples Anonymous (RCA)
P.O. Box 11029
Oakland, CA 94611
Tel: (510) 663-2312
Web: www.recovering-couples.org

Sex Addicts Anonymous (SAA)
P.O. Box 70949
Houston, TX 77270
Tel: (800) 477-8191
Web: www.sexaa.org

Sex and Love Addicts Anonymous (SLAA)
1550 Northeast Loop 410, Suite 118
San Antonio, TX 78206
Tel: (210) 828-7900
Web: www.slaafws.org

Appendix C
RECOMMENDED READING LIST

PART OF A SOUND RECOVERY PROGRAM should include accessing the works of various authors whose fields of expertise relate to your addiction. The works listed here cover topics from sexual compulsivity to borderline personality disorder (BPD).

Carnes, Patrick. *Don't Call It Love: Recovery from Sexual Addiction.* New York: Bantam Books, 1992. This is an excellent book to consider if you are seeking help for a sexual addiction. Dr. Carnes uncovered something very taboo in today's society that had needed attention for some time.

Guerrero, Laura K., Peter Andersen, and Walid Afifi. *Close Encounters: Communicating in Relationships.* New York: McGraw-Hill, 2001. Written by three very wise authors, this college textbook offers a modern approach to understanding how and why people relate in personal relationships. I use this textbook for my course in interpersonal communications.

Jackson, Quinn Tyler. *Janus Incubus.* Whales, UK: Plane Tree Publications, 2002. The struggles of BPD are revealed in this fast-moving novel. At the time of this book's publication, Jackson was nominated for an American Psychological Association's Distinguished Scientific Award. A must-read for people who believe they suffer from BPD and confuse love with obsession.

Lewis, Judith A. *Addictions: Concepts and Strategies for Treatment*. Gaithersburg, MD: Aspen, 1994. Lewis's textbook covers various kinds of addictions. It uncovers the sociological and familial role of the addictions process with unique insight from an expert.

Norwood, Robin. *Women Who Love Too Much: When You Keep Wishing and Hoping He'll Change*. New York: Pocket Books, 1990. Norwood's book truly is a classic. A former therapist, she uncovers the problem of relational addiction with an emphasis on women. But don't let the title fool you. Women who love too much is appropriate for both sexes and offers unique insight from a very gifted writer.

INDEX

abandonment
  during childhood, 17–18,
    52, 61, 65, 115–16
  emotional, 19–20
  fear of, 16, 18, 25, 52, 61, 63,
    89, 112, 115, 133, 167
abuse
  during childhood, 15, 17–18,
    19–21, 32, 127, 158
  emotional, 19–20, 67,
    116–19
  fear of, 67, 82–83
  financial, 21, 22, 51–53,
    58–60, 64–65
  generational, 118
  justifying, 67, 75, 80
  physical. *See* physical abuse
  relational effects of, 45–46,
    68, 78, 79–83, 118–19
  in relationships, 17, 28–29,
    67–76, 82–83
  sexual, 127–28
addiction, 99
  bio-psychosocial model of,
    68
  "bottoming out" in, 44–45,
    99–100, 111

childhood experiences and,
  68
diagnostic criteria
  for, 101–2
disease model of, 104,
  107–8, 109, 155, 163
of parents, 20, 32, 112,
  115–16, 118
to a relationship. *See* relational dependency (RD)
sexual. *See* sexual
  addiction
See also coaddiction
Addictions (Lewis), 68
affirmations, 170, 179–80
alcohol, as tool of control,
  119–24
alcoholism, 80
American Psychiatric
  Association, 4, 101
anger, 82, 155, 156, 159
anxiety, 25, 133–34, 154

bio-psychology, 68
blame, 80, 155, 164, 171
borderline personality
  disorder, 4

therapists, 8, 68, 104, 164–66
  locating, 166
trauma, 87–88, 89, 90

validation, 97, 123, 144
Victorian Institute of Forensic
  Mental Health, 46

withdrawal symptoms, 98–99,
  135
*Women Who Love Too Much:
When You Keep Wishing and
Hoping He'll Change*
  (Norwood), 52
work histories, 26, 42–43

About the Author

JOHN D. MOORE, M.S., is an associate professor of health sciences at American Military University and is a licensed clinical professional counselor in the state of Illinois with board certification in alcohol and drug counseling. In addition to his teaching responsibilities, Moore is a psychotherapist in private practice and is the former group leader of a support group for the relationally dependent. His seminal contributions on the topic of addiction and relationships appear regularly in nationally syndicated magazines, and he lectures widely on the topic of love. A native of Chicago, Moore lives on the city's North Side.

OTHER TITLES THAT MAY INTEREST YOU:

Codependent No More
How to Stop Controlling Others and Start Caring for Yourself
Melody Beattie
Is someone else's problem your problem? If so, you may be codependent—and you may find yourself in this book. This modern classic holds the key to understanding codependency and charts a path to a lifetime of healing, hope, and happiness. Softcover, 264 pp.
Order No. 5014

Is It Love or Is It Addiction?
Second Edition
Brenda Schaeffer
This book has helped countless people find their way from the trials and confusions of addictive love to the fulfillment of whole and healthy relationships. If offers a fresh perspective on intimacy and practical advice on making relationships work. Softcover, 216 pp.
Order No. 5686

Stop Hurting the Woman You Love
Breaking the Cycle of Abusive Behavior
Charlie Donaldson, M.A., Randy Flood, M.A., with
    Elaine Eldridge, Ph.D.
The authors help men understand why they emotionally and physically hurt their partners, identify practical strategies to avoid domestic abuse, and develop a plan to create more satisfying relationships. Softcover, 224 pp.
Order No. 2608

Hazelden

Hazelden books are available at fine bookstores everywhere. To order directly from Hazelden, call 1-800-328-9000 or visit www.hazelden.org/bookstore.